Heroes in American Folklore

ILLUSTRATED

BY

JAMES DAUGHERTY

AND

DONALD McKAY

Heroes
in
American
Folklore

BY

IRWIN SHAPIRO

JULIAN MESSNER
New York

Published simultaneously in the United States and Canada by
Julian Messner, a division of Simon & Schuster, Inc.,
1 West 39 Street, New York, N.Y. 10018. All rights reserved.

Sixth Printing, 1973

Printed in the United States of America
ISBN 0-671-32054-8 MCE
Library of Congress Catalog Card No. 62-10205

CONTENTS

CASEY JONES
AND LOCOMOTIVE NO. 638

STORY BY IRWIN SHAPIRO

PICTURES BY DONALD McKAY

THERE's always been a Jones on the railroad. And the greatest of them all was Casey Jones.

Casey couldn't help being a railroad man. He was born to the long, lonesome wail of a locomotive whistle. He grew up to the sound of the engine moan. He started out as a call boy, then was a ticket agent, a telegraph operator, a brakeman, and a fireman. At last he got to be an engineer, and drove a big eight-wheeler of a mighty fame.

Yes, everybody knows Casey was a great engineer. Everybody knows the song about Casey. Everybody *doesn't* know that the song jumps the track when it says Casey was killed in the wreck of Locomotive No. 638. Because the truth is, there wasn't any wreck. The truth is, Casey almost didn't even get near No. 638. The truth is that Casey liked to play baseball, and—well, here's what really happened.

It all goes back to the day the east-bound limited was rolling along toward Chicago. Casey was sitting in the cab of Locomotive No. 4. He was wearing high-bibbed overalls and a red thousand-mile shirt. He had a black engineer's cap on his head, and a blue bandanna handkerchief around his neck for a sweat rag.

As they rattled over a crossing, Casey checked the time on his gold stem-winding watch. After that he picked up his long-necked copper oil can and put a drop of oil on his handle-bar mustache.

"Nothing like a little prime, pure en-jine oil to give whiskers a gloss," he said to the fireman.

Pulling into the depot at Chicago, Casey played his whippoorwill call on the whistle. And when he did, the folks at the depot stopped whatever they were doing. The baggage-smashers stopped handling baggage. The telegraph

operators stopped pounding brass. The station agent stopped selling tickets, and the passengers stopped buying tickets. For they knew the man at the throttle was Casey Jones.

A crowd of Joneses came rushing up to the locomotive. With them was Casey's uncle, old Memphis Jones. Uncle Memphis had been an engineer himself, and he still wore a black engineer's cap. At the end of every run he was always on hand with a crowd of other Joneses to give Casey a cheer.

"There he is!" said Uncle Memphis proudly.

"Hurray for Casey!" shouted the Joneses. "Hurray for Casey Jones!"

Casey swung himself off the cab, giving the crowd a wave of the hand.

"How's the old pitching arm?" asked Uncle Memphis.

"Strong and limber and ready to pitch," answered Casey.

"How about showing us your new razzle-dazzler?" said the Joneses.

"Glad to obleege," said Casey.

Uncle Memphis handed Casey a baseball and a pitcher's glove. He stood off from Casey, put on a catcher's mitt, and gave Casey the signal. Casey wound up and let the ball fly.

The ball swung out in a big curve. Then it took three little hops. Then it twisted around like a corkscrew, and bam! hit the catcher's mitt.

"That's pitching!" yelled the Joneses. "Sure is a razzle-dazzler!"

"Baseball—hm!" said a deep voice behind Casey, and Casey turned around.

There stood a little fat man with bushy eyebrows. He was wearing a derby hat and a stand-up collar. He had a diamond stick-pin in his tie, and he was carrying a gold-handled cane.

"Well, well," said Casey. "If it's not Bolsun Brown, Superintendent of the Central Pacific Railroad."

Before Bolsun could open his mouth to speak, Casey held up his hand.

"Same old Bolsun," said Casey. "First thing you'll do is tell me it doesn't look right to pitch ball on the platform of the depot."

Bolsun tapped his cane on the ground. But he didn't say a word.

"After that," said Casey, "you'll tell me it doesn't look right for an engineer to play baseball."

Once again Bolsun didn't say a word.

"Then," said Casey, "you'll tell me baseball and railroading don't mix."

Still Bolsun didn't say a word.

"And you'll end up," said Casey, "by telling me I ought to give up baseball. And if I don't, I'll lose my touch on the throttle."

Bolsun cleared his throat and said, "Casey, it's true it doesn't look right for you to play baseball. But I'm not saying so. It's true baseball and railroading don't mix. But I'm not saying that, either. It's true you ought to give it up, and it's true you'll lose your touch on the throttle. But that's something else I'm not saying."

Casey looked at Bolsun.

"Maybe it's not the same old Bolsun after all," he said. "You sure you're not going to say any ot those things?"

"Not one," said Bolsun. "All I've got to say is this— I'd like to show you something at the World's Fair Exposition."

Casey asked Uncle Memphis if there was anything at the Exposition for a railroad man to see.

"Couldn't say," answered Uncle Memphis. "I haven't had time to go there. I haven't even read about it in the paper. I've been too busy working out the batting averages of your baseball team."

"Guess it won't do any harm to take a look at it," said Casey, and the three of them left the depot.

It was evening when they got to the Exposition grounds. Crowds of people walked between the white buildings. Colored lights were strung everywhere. Fountains spurted. Gondolas floated on the big lake. Bands played music, and fireworks exploded in the sky.

The Midway of the Exposition was lined with the tents of side-shows. Barkers shouted, "R-r-r-right this way, folks! The big show is about to begin! Don't miss it! Only ten cents—one dime—the tenth part of a dollar. Hurry, hurry, hurry!"

But Bolsun wouldn't let Casey and Uncle Memphis see the side-shows. He wouldn't let them see the sword swallower,

the midgets, or the human skeleton. He hustled them straight to a big white building, with a golden arch and golden letters that said:

HALL OF TRANSPORTATION

Inside the building, Bolsun pulled them away from an old Stevenson locomotive and a bright new Pullman car.

"That's not what I wanted to show you," he said. Then he pointed with his gold-handled cane and said, "But *that* is."

On a little spur of track stood a new locomotive. She was a big eight-wheeler, the biggest ever built. She had the longest

driving-rod ever made. Her black paint was as dark as the inside of a tunnel, and her brass bell shone like a light. She was decked out in flags and red-white-and-blue bunting. Propped up against her was a sign:

LOCOMOTIVE NO. 638

Built on the order
of
Superintendent Bolsun Brown
for the
CENTRAL PACIFIC RAILROAD

Casey walked all around No. 638. He looked her over, and he looked her under, and he looked her every which way.

"That *is* a smokeolotive," he said.

"I'm not denying it," said Bolsun.

"That is a hog," said Uncle Memphis.

"I'm not disputing it," said Bolsun.

"Makes old No. 4 look like a hay-burner," said Casey.

"I'm not saying she doesn't," said Bolsun.

Bolsun leaned back on his gold-handled cane.

"Casey," he said, "how would you like to put your hand on her throttle? How would you like to play your whippoorwill call on her whistle? How would you like to sit in her cab and watch her drivers roll?"

"I can see her now," said Casey, "highballing along, breaking all records. I can see her now."

"Casey," said Bolsun quickly, "you give up baseball, and I'll let you take out No. 638. I'll give you the right-of-way from Chicago to 'Frisco, and you can break all records."

"Why, Bolsun," said Uncle Memphis, "you couldn't

17

give No. 638 to anybody *else*. Nobody but a Jones could handle her, and Casey's the only Jones on the railroad."

"I don't know about that," said Bolsun. "A Brown could handle her. I used to be an engineer myself, and I'd take the run if I wasn't Superintendent."

Casey and Uncle Memphis burst out laughing. Uncle Memphis snorted and said, "Bolsun, you're a good Superintendent. But you never were much of an engineer. Casey is the only man around to take out No. 638. You'll never get him to give up baseball that way."

"Just a minute," said Casey. "I'd like to obleege you, Bolsun. And I'd like to take out No. 638. I'll tell you what I'll do; if my baseball team loses the game next week, I'll give up baseball."

"But your team never loses," said Bolsun, frowning. "You know—"

Suddenly Bolsun stopped. He walked a few steps up and down, tapping with his gold-handled cane. Then the frown left his face and he held out his hand.

"I'll take you up on that," he said. "If your team loses, you'll give up baseball. And I'll give you the right-of-way to 'Frisco with No. 638."

"Don't do it, Casey!" shouted Uncle Memphis. "Don't

take him up on it! He's got some trick thought up to make you lose the game!"

"The only trick he could do," said Casey, "is to find the other team a pitcher like me. But there's only one Casey Jones. I'll take you up on that, Bolsun."

Bolsun and Casey shook hands. They had another look at No. 638, then left the Exposition grounds together. Bolsun went to his house, and Casey and Uncle Memphis went to their rooms at Mrs. Callahan's Rooming House for Railroad men.

All that week Casey took out old No. 4. The day of the game he brought her into the depot the way he always did. He put a drop of engine oil on his handle-bar mustache to give it a gloss, and headed straight for the ball park.

Soon as Casey came out on the field, his catcher said, "You're just in time. Better get into your uniform and warm up."

"I don't need any uniform," said Casey. "And I don't

need to warm up. My arm is still warm from en-jine heat."

The next minute the umpire held up his hand.

"Bat-tries for today's game!" he shouted, "For Casey Jones's Tigers—Casey Jones and Smith! For the South Side Wildcats—Hallahan and Hoke! Play ball!"

Casey walked out to the pitcher's mound, while the folks gave him a cheer. On one side of the stands sat the Wildcat rooters. On the other side sat the Tiger rooters. With them was Uncle Memphis, and almost every Jones in the city of Chicago. And sitting squeezed in between the Wildcat rooters and the Tiger rooters was Bolsun Brown.

"Let's go!" cried the Tiger rooters. "Give 'em the old razzle-dazzler, Casey!"

"Come on, you Wildcats!" said the Wildcat rooters. "Knock Casey out of the box!"

Bolsun Brown didn't cheer with the Tigers or the Wildcats. He just sat there, watching Casey from under his bushy eyebrows. His hands were folded over his gold-handled cane, and his chin rested on his hands.

"Batter up!" shouted the umpire, and the game was on.

The first seven innings, Casey didn't allow the Wildcats a hit. He made three home runs himself, scoring two men. The score was five to nothing, favor the Tigers.

At the beginning of the eighth inning, Casey winked at Bolsun. Bolsun just kept sitting there, the way he had.

"I knew Bolsun couldn't keep me from winning," said Casey to himself. He got the signal from the catcher, wound up, and threw a curve.

"Stur-r-r-r-i-i-ike!" said the umpire.

Casey got the ball again and threw a straight fast one.

"Ball!" said the umpire.

The batter missed Casey's next pitch by a mile.

"Strike tuh!" said the um-pire.

The pitch after that was a little close.

"Ball tuh!" said the umpire. "Tuh and tuh!"

The next two were high and a little wide.

"Ball thu-ree!" said the umpire. "Thu-ree and tuh! Thu-ree and tuh!"

The catcher tossed the ball to the first baseman. The first baseman tossed it to the second baseman. The second base-man tossed it to the shortstop. The shortstop tossed it to the third baseman, who tossed it to the catcher. The catcher walked over to Casey and handed him the ball. Before he went back behind the plate, he whispered something in Casey's ear. Casey whispered something back and nodded.

"Take him out!" yelled the Wildcat rooters. "He's up in the air! He's up in the air!"

"Give him the old razzle-dazzler, Casey!" yelled the Tiger rooters. "Strike him out!"

"Play ball!" said the umpire.

Casey leaned way back, wound way up, and let the ball fly. First it swung out in a big curve. Then it took three little hops. Then it twisted around like a corkscrew, and bam! hit the catcher's mitt.

"Ball!" said the umpire. "Ball four! Take ya base!"

"Boo!" said the Tiger rooters. "Robber! Blind man! Get him a tin cup!"

Before the batter could even throw down his bat, Bolsun Brown hopped out of the stands. He waved his gold-handled cane in the air. He jumped up and down. And he ran out on the field, bellowing, "What's that you said, umpire?"

"Ball four," said the umpire.

"Why, you wall-eyed swindler!" roared Bolsun. "That ball was right over the plate!"

Both teams came crowding around Bolsun and the umpire. Everybody except Casey was talking and shouting and waving his hands.

Bolsun pushed Casey close to the umpire.

"Go ahead, Casey!" he yelled. "Tell him! Tell this blind man!"

"Just what are you going to tell me?" the umpire asked Casey.

"That ball was right over the plate!" said Bolsun.

"Oh, you do, do you?" said the umpire to Casey.

"Yes, he does!" said Bolsun.

Bolsun and the umpire went on shouting. Each of them looked at Casey, and Casey looked at each of them. Casey's head kept going back and forth, but he didn't say anything. He couldn't get a word in edgewise.

"I'm the umpire," said the umpire, pushing back his little blue cap. "I calls 'em as I sees 'em. And I sees this ball as high and a little close. Now play ball!"

"Play ball nothing!" said Bolsun, pushing back his derby. "You called that one wrong and you know it! That's what Casey is telling you!"

By this time the umpire was red in the face. He leaned close to Casey and he poked him with his finger.

"I repeats," he said, "I'm the umpire."

"Casey knows you're the umpire," snapped Bolsun.

"I repeats," said the umpire, "I calls 'em as I sees 'em."

"How can you see 'em?" said Bolsun. "You're blind in one eye and wall-eyed in the other."

"And I repeats," said the umpire, "I sees this as a little high and a little close. Now are you going to play ball?"

"Not until you call that a strike," said Bolsun. "Casey's not playing ball till you call it a strike."

"No pitcher can talk that way to me!" shouted the umpire.

"You're being talked to that way right now," said Bolsun.

"Then get off the field!" roared the umpire at Casey. "Get off the field! Because I calls 'em as I sees 'em, and no pitcher can talk that way to me! Now get off the field, put in another pitcher, and let's PLAY BALL!"

"Look here, umpire—" Casey began.

"I've heard enough out of you!" bellowed the umpire. "One more word, and I'll give the game to the Wildcats!"

"Better do what he says, Casey," said Bolsun.

And while the rooters in the stands yelled and howled, Casey went back to the bench. Bolsun walked beside him, swinging his gold-handled cane so that it caught the shine of the sun.

"You shouldn't have done that, Casey," said Bolsun. "You shouldn't have talked that way to the umpire."

Bolsun put his derby on straight. He looked sadly at Casey, and shook his head. He walked out of the ball park, shaking his head as he went. Casey put in another pitcher, and the game went on.

Of course the other pitcher couldn't hold the Wildcats. They scored eight runs that inning, batting clear around the batting order. Casey sent in still another pitcher, but he didn't do much good either. The inning ended with the Wildcats leading fifteen to five.

Then Casey's team came up to bat. The Wildcats put them out so fast Casey hardly knew what was happening. The game was over, and his team had lost.

Casey left the ball park with Uncle Memphis and a crowd of Joneses.

"It's a sad day for the Joneses," they sighed.

"It is, and yet it isn't," said Casey. "Because I was tricked."

"What do you mean?" asked Uncle Memphis. "Didn't you talk back to the umpire?"

"Didn't say a word," said Casey. "Didn't get a chance to."

He told the Joneses what had happened, and they all agreed he'd been tricked.

"All the same, it's a sad day for the Joneses," said the Joneses. "A Jones has been out-smarted by a Brown."

"But not for long!" roared Uncle Memphis. "Casey, you come along with me. We're going to pay a little visit to Superintendent Bolsun Brown."

Casey and Uncle Memphis went to the depot. They went up to the top floor of the depot building, and into Bolsun Brown's office. Before they could see Bolsun, they had to see his junior clerk, his senior clerk, his secretary's secretary, and his secretary. But at last they saw Bolsun himself.

"Good afternoon, gentlemen," said Bolsun.

He was sitting in a swivel chair, with his feet up on his rolltop desk.

"Glad to see you," he said. "Glad you dropped around. If you hadn't called on me, I would have called on you. Because I'd like to remind you, Casey, of our little agreement. You said if you lost the ball game, you'd give up baseball. Yes, you said you'd give up baseball and stick to railroading.

Remember?"

"I remember," said Casey.

"And," said Bolsun, "you lost the ball game this afternoon. Remember?"

"And now you remember something," said Casey. "I didn't lose that ball game. I was tricked."

"Casey's right," put in Uncle Memphis. "You got him thrown out of the game. And he's not going to give up baseball."

Bolsun jumped to his feet.

"You mean to say you're not going to give up baseball?" he said, glaring at Casey.

"That's exactly what I mean," answered Casey.

"Casey," said Bolsun slowly, "I mean it for your own good. Baseball and railroading don't mix. If you go on playing ball, you'll lose your touch on the throttle."

"Maybe they don't mix for a Brown, but they mix for a

Jones!" shouted Casey. "Don't you tell me what's good for me! I was tricked, and I'm not going to quit playing ball."

"Then you'll never drive another locomotive for me!" shouted back Bolsun. "You'll never drive No. 638, No. 4, or any other hog on this line. From now on, Casey, you'll be the telegraph operator at the Oak Park station!"

"Me go back to pounding brass?" said Casey.

"Yes, you! And you'll be night operator, so you can play baseball all day! And when you get tired of pounding brass, maybe you'll give up baseball. And maybe then I'll let you go back to being an engineer."

"You can't do that to Casey Jones!" said Uncle Memphis.

"No, sir!" said Casey. "I quit!"

Bolsun sat down again in his swivel chair. He put his feet up on his rolltop desk, and he smiled.

"Oh, no," he said. "I'm not letting you go to another railroad. You're a good engineer, Casey. And if you stop playing baseball, you'll be one of the best. And I don't think you'll quit. Because if you do, I won't give you your clearance papers. And without your clearance papers you'll never get a job on any railroad. No, there won't be a Jones on any railroad at all. Good day, Mr. Memphis Jones. Good day, Casey.

Don't forget to report to work at the Oak Park station."

And that night Casey went back to pounding brass. He put away his high-bibbed overalls and his red thousand-mile shirt. He put away his black engineer's cap and his blue bandanna handkerchief. He wore a blue serge suit just like anybody else, with a white shirt and blue tie.

Of course Casey could pound brass with the best of them, and he kept the wires humming. Besides pounding the brass, he set the signal lights. If a train was to go ahead, he'd set the signal light on the green. If a train had to stop for orders, he'd set the signal light red. Then the engineer would stop his train and pick up his orders from Casey.

Night after night Casey sat all alone in the little station. It made him sad to listen to the long, lonesome wail of the locomotive whistles. It made him sad to listen to their engines moan. But he wouldn't give up playing baseball. He knew baseball would never make a Jones lose his touch on the throttle. And he knew he'd been tricked by Bolsun Brown.

One night Uncle Memphis came into the station, where
Casey was pounding brass.

"Casey," said Uncle Memphis, "how long is this going to
go on?"

Casey didn't know, and he said so.

"It's got to stop," said Uncle Memphis. "Do you know
what's happening? The Browns are laughing at the Joneses.
All over the city of Chicago, and way beyond. Bolsun is
going around telling the Browns how he tricked you, and
they're laughing their heads off."

"They can't do that," said Casey angrily. "Nobody has
ever laughed at the Joneses before."

"They're doing it," said Uncle Memphis. "They're doing
it. And there's only one thing left for you to do."

"What's that?" asked Casey.

"Bolsun tricked you, and you've got to trick him back," answered Uncle Memphis.

"But how, Uncle Memphis? How?"

"That's why I came here tonight," said Uncle Memphis. "You just leave everything to me."

"Go right ahead," said Casey. "When do you start."

"Right now," said Uncle Memphis.

The first thing Uncle Memphis did was to take the plugs out of the main trunk wires. After that he took the switch keys out of the telegraph stand. The telegraph stopped clacking, leaving the room quiet.

"That takes care of the telegraph," said Uncle Memphis.

The next thing he did was set the signal lights red, for both the east bound trains and the west bound trains.

"That takes care of the signal lights," he said.

Uncle Memphis told Casey to put on his hat and hand over the keys. Then they both stepped outside. Uncle Memphis locked the door of the station and said, "And that takes care of Bolsun Brown."

"I'm beginning to think it will," said Casey.

Outside the rails stretched east and west, shining in the light of the moon. Above the rails shone the red signal lights. Uncle Memphis looked around and pulled Casey into the bushes at the side of the tracks.

"We'll just wait here for a little while," he said. "Soon you'll see something worth seeing."

They didn't wait long before the west bound express came roaring up. When the engineer saw the red light, he pulled up in front of the station. He jumped down from the cab, went to the station, and rattled the door knob. The door wouldn't open, so he looked in the window. And what he saw made him take off his cap and scratch his head.

33

Then the conductor hopped off the train, together with a brakeman.

"Nobody here," Casey and Uncle Memphis heard the engineer say.

"There's got to be," said the conductor.

"See for yourself," said the engineer. "And we can't go on till we get the green light."

While the engineer was talking, the east bound limited pulled up at the station. The engineer jumped down from the cab and walked over to the other trainmen. And while they talked to him, the east bound local and the west bound freight pulled up. In no time at all there was a little crowd of trainmen standing in front of the station. Passengers looked out the windows of the cars, asking what was holding them up. The brakemen lit red lanterns, and the locomotives puffed steam.

"Guess you've seen enough to get the idea," said Uncle Memphis to Casey. "Now we'll go up to the Trainmen's Tavern."

The Trainmen's Tavern was on a little hill above the station. The back room was crowded with Joneses. Some of them were at the window, looking at the tie-up on the railroad. Others sat around the tables, which were loaded down with sandwiches, cider, and ale. When they saw Casey and Uncle Memphis they raised a cheer.

"It's a fine night for the Joneses," they said.

"But not for the Browns," said Uncle Memphis. "Especially not for Bolsun Brown." He picked up a glass of cider and sang:

> There's a red light on the track for
> Bolsun Brown, Bolsun Brown,
> There's a red light on the track for
> Bolsun Brown.
> There's a red light on the track,
> And it'll be there when he gets back,
> There's a red light on the track for
> Bolsun Brown.

"Sure is," laughed Casey, pointing out the window.

Uncle Memphis and the other Joneses looked down. Below them trains were piled up as far as they could see. There were east bound trains and west bound trains. There were express trains, local trains, freight trains, and a few locomotives with just a tender and a caboose. Whistles were blowing and steam was hissing. In the glare of the headlights trainmen and passengers ran around. They shouted to each other and waved their arms. Every once in a while they'd point to the red signal lights, still shining above the tracks. It was the biggest tie-up in the history of railroads.

"Look at that smoke coming out of those smokestacks!" said the Joneses.

"That's a pretty sight," said Casey.

"Listen to those whistles blow!" said the Joneses.

"Sounds like music to me," said Casey.

The Joneses started to sing:

> The wind it blew up the railroad tracks,
> It blew, It blew.
> The wind it blew up the railroad tracks,
> It blew way up and half way back,
> By Jiminy! How it blew!
> By Jiminy! How it blew!

Uncle Memphis pulled out his gold stem-winding watch and said, "The news must have got to Bolsun by this time. Guess he'll soon be paying us a little visit."

It wasn't more than two minutes later that Bolsun burst into the room. He was puffing and out of breath. His derby was pushed over to one side of his head, and his stick-pin was stuck crooked in his tie.

"Casey," he puffed, "thought—puff, puff—I'd—puff, puff —find you—puff, puff—here."

"Glad you did," said Casey. "Won't you step in and join the fun?"

"That's right," said the Joneses. "Have a glass of cider, Bolsun. Have a sandwich."

Bolsun's eyebrows came down over his eyes. His hand shook on his gold-handled cane.

"What's the trouble?" asked Casey, as polite as you please.

"You know very well what's the trouble!" shouted Bolsun. "You can hear those whistles blowing! You can hear that steam hissing! You can see those trains piled up, waiting for the green light to go ahead!"

Bolsun took a deep breath and roared, "Casey, give me

the keys to the station! I'm the Superintendent of this railroad, and I order you to give me those keys!"

Casey took a sip of cider.

"I'd like to obleege you, Bolsun," he said. "But first you'll have to answer a question or two."

"Such as?" asked Bolsun.

"Such as this," answered Casey. "Will you put me back on a locomotive?"

"No!" howled Bolsun.

"Then will you give me my clearance papers, so's I can get a job on another railroad?"

"No!" bellowed Bolsun.

"No keys," said Casey.

"May as well get back to our fun," said Uncle Memphis. He and the other Joneses started singing *There's a Red Light on the Track for Bolsun Brown*.

Bolsun was white in the face. Above the singing he could hear the whistles blowing and the steam hissing.

"All right," he said at last. "All right, Casey. I won't put you back on a locomotive. But I'll give you your clearance papers. You'll get them in the mail in the morning."

Uncle Memphis handed the keys to Bolsun, and Bolsun snatched them up.

"Well, Casey," said Bolsun. "You've got your clearance papers. But you'll never drive a locomotive again! Because I'll see that the story of what you did gets around! And no railroad will hire a man that started a tie-up! Then you'll come begging to me. But I'll never give you a job! And there won't be any Jones on the railroad at all!"

"Now, Bolsun," said Uncle Memphis. "You know you'll take Casey back. He's the only engineer who can handle No. 638."

"Ha!" laughed Bolsun. "The railroad can get along without a Jones. I'll handle No. 638 myself. Casey won't even get near her! If Casey ever sets foot in her cab, I'll quit my job as Superintendent! Then Casey can run the whole railroad! But he won't! And there will never be a Jones on the railroad again!"

With that he slammed the door and left. The Joneses looked at each other. Some of them began to say maybe it wasn't such a fine night for the Joneses after all. But Casey wasn't worried.

The next morning Casey got his clearance papers. Once again he put on his red thousand-mile shirt and his high-bibbed overalls. Once again he put his black engineer's cap on his head, and a blue bandanna around his neck for a sweat rag. He put a drop of oil on his handle-bar mustache to give it a gloss, and set off.

Casey went straight to the depot of the Illinois Central Railroad. He walked into the superintendent's office, showed his clearance papers, and asked for a job.

"Afraid not," was the superintendent's answer. "We know you're a good engineer. There's nothing wrong with your clearance papers. But we heard about that tie-up yesterday on the Central Pacific. We couldn't take a chance on a man who'd do something like that."

Casey saw that Bolsun had been right. There wasn't a railroad in the country that would give him a job. As he walked back to Mrs. Callahan's Rooming House for Railroad Men, he looked sad. His feet shuffled and his head hung low. But as soon as he was in the front parlor with Uncle Memphis, he began to smile.

"What's there to smile about?" asked Uncle Memphis after Casey had told him what happened. "Have you seen this?"

He shoved a newspaper into Casey's hand. On the second page was a big notice:

TWO WEEKS FROM TONIGHT

First run of the Cannon Ball Express
from Chicago to San Francisco
with

LOCOMOTIVE NO. 638

Leaves the Chicago Depot at 8:52

The Cannon Ball will have the
right of way and will attempt
to break all speed records

ENGINEER—SUPERINTENDENT BOLSUN BROWN

"Bolsun can't handle No. 638," said Uncle Memphis.

"And he's not going to," said Casey. "Because I'm going to be in the cab of that locomotive."

"What's your plan?" asked Uncle Memphis.

"Never mind that now," said Casey. "You go around looking sad. You tell all the other Joneses to look sad. But on the night No. 638 makes her run, you and the other Joneses buy yourselves a round-trip ticket to 'Frisco. You get on board the Cannon Ball, and you'll see some real railroading."

Uncle Memphis wasn't so sure. Still, he did what Casey told him. He went around looking sad. He kept saying, "Never thought I'd see the day when there wasn't a Jones on the railroad." And all the other Joneses looked so sad even the Browns felt sorry for them.

Casey looked sadder than any of them. On the day No. 638 was to make her run, he dropped in at the Blue Front Restaurant. Bolsun Brown was sitting at the counter. Casey sat down himself, giving a little moan.

"What'll it be, Casey," asked the counterman. "You name it—I've got it."

"I'm not hungry," said Casey. "I'll just have a Trainmen's Delight."

"Trainmen's Delight," repeated the counterman. He gave Casey a T-bone steak, with French fried potatoes and cream gravy.

"Lost your appetite?" asked Bolsun.

"Kind of," said Casey.

"Sorry to hear it," said Bolsun. "How come you're not out playing baseball on a nice day like this."

"Can't get my heart in it," said Casey.

"Too bad," said Bolsun. "Too bad when a man can't play ball or railroad."

Casey sighed.

"Bolsun," he said, "if I bought a ticket could I ride on the Cannon Ball tonight?"

Bolsun threw back his head and laughed.

"Oh, no, Casey," he said: "You're not even going to get near No. 638. Memphis can ride, and any other Jones, if they want to. But not you, Casey. Can't take chances. I'm going to have guards all around. You'll have to read about it in the paper."

"That's what I thought," said Casey slowly.

He finished his Trainmen's Delight, then went back to the rooming house. He stayed there until it was night, and when he came out again nobody would have known it was Casey.

Because Casey had shaved off his mustache. His face was covered with soot and coal dust. He was wearing somebody else's overalls, and somebody else's thousand-mile shirt. He had an old banged-up oil can in his pocket and he didn't have any watch at all.

Casey made his way to the depot, where No. 638 was

getting up steam. She was still decked out in flags and red-white-and-blue bunting. She was clean and shining and ready to go. A few hostlers were still working over her, wiping off a few specks of dust.

Casey pushed his way through the crowd and saw the bright new cars behind No. 638. People were getting on, waving good-by. Among them was Uncle Memphis and the Joneses. A guard at the door of each car watched them, to make sure Casey wasn't trying to sneak on.

Then Casey saw Bolsun Brown. He wasn't wearing his derby, and he wasn't carrying his gold-handled cane. He had on brand new engineer's clothes, and he carried his orders in his hand. After Bolsun started talking to the conductor, Casey hurried to the locomotive. There was a whole ring of guards around No. 638, but they let Casey through.

Casey climbed up to the cab. He poked the fireman with
his finger and said, "Seems there's been a mistake."

"What kind of mistake?" asked the fireman. His face was
covered with soot and coal dust, just like Casey's.

"Seems you weren't supposed to be the fireman on this
run," said Casey. "Seems that I was."

"But I got my call from the call boy!" said the fireman.

"He's the one who made the mistake," said Casey. "Got
everything all twisted up. Bolsun Brown just found out and
told me I was to be the fireman on this hog."

"Guess I'd better go, then," said the fireman.

"That's right," said Casey. "And don't let Bolsun see
you. He's angry enough as it is."

The fireman climbed down, and Casey picked up his
shovel. He was shoveling away when Bolsun mounted to the
cab. Casey kept his face turned away from Bolsun and kept
on shoveling coal.

"Looks bad," said Bolsun in a squeaky voice. "There are

storms all along the way. There are washouts and landslides. Looks bad."

"I'm not worried," said Casey. "Can't anything stop a Brown."

Casey went on shoveling coal till he heard the conductor yell, "Board! All a-boar-r-rd!"

"There's the brakeman giving us the highball," said Bolsun. "Jingle the brass, fireman."

Casey pulled the cord of the bell. Bolsun opened the throttle, and No. 638 began to pull out.

"Chug-chug-chug!" went her engine. Then it went Sssssssssssst! and stopped.

Bolsun's hand was shaking on the throttle.

"Maybe I've lost my touch," he said.

"How come?" asked Casey. "Have you been playing base-ball?"

"Why, no," said Bolsun. "What makes you say that?"

"Always heard baseball made an engineer lose his touch," answered Casey.

Bolsun wiped his face with his sweat rag and tried again. This time No. 638 roared out of the depot. The only trouble was, she didn't run smooth. She rattled and wheezed and swung from side to side. She didn't run fast at all. When Bolsun tried to blow her whistle, all he got was a little peep.

"Well, we're on our way," said Bolsun, trying to smile.

"Sure are," said Casey, trying *not* to smile.

It wasn't long before they ran into the storm. The rain poured down. The thunder made a noise louder than No. 638. Every once in a while lightning flashed down, striking a tree or pole along the tracks.

Suddenly Bolsun let out a yell and stopped the train.

"Look!" he said.

Right below them was a deep valley. There was a trestle bridge over the valley, but it had been struck by lightning. Now it was burning, and soon there wouldn't be any bridge at all.

"Can't cross through that fire," said Bolsun. "And we can't cross without any bridge. I guess we'd better turn back. We'll never get to 'Frisco tonight."

The conductor and a brakeman ran up to the locomotive to see what was stopping them. They saw the trestle bridge burning, and they said the same thing as Bolsun.

"Casey Jones could get her through," said Casey quietly.

"Don't think he could," said the conductor. "And he's not anywhere near No. 638."

"Look here, fireman," said Bolsun, "I've heard enough talk about Casey Jones."

"And you're going to hear a lot more!" shouted Casey, wiping the soot and coal dust off his face with his sweat rag. He stepped close to Bolsun and opened the fire door. The engine fire lit up his face so that Bolsun could see it.

"You couldn't be!" said Bolsun. "You can't . . . ! You're not . . . ! But you are Casey Jones!"

"Casey Jones it is," said Casey. "Don't have my handle-bar mustache, but the rest of me is here. Bolsun, do you remember what you said the night of the tie-up? Remember how you said if I set foot in the cab of No. 638 I could have your job?"

Bolsun sank back into the fireman's seat.

"You win, Casey," he said. "I don't know how you did it, but you're here. I remember what I said and I won't go back on my word. You're the new Superintendent of the Central Pacific Railroad." Then he jumped up and shouted,

"But if you think you can get this train to 'Frisco you're crazy!"

"That's no way to talk to the Superintendent of this railroad," said Casey. He ordered the conductor and the brakeman to board the train. A cheer came from the Joneses when they heard the news.

Casey sat down on the engineer's seat and put his hand on the throttle. He pulled the whistle cord, and blew his whippoorwill call on the whistle. Then he put the engine into reverse, and the train started rolling backward.

"Ha!" said Bolsun. "I knew it! I knew it! You're taking her back!"

"Just hold on there, Bolsun," said Casey. "You'll see what I'm going to do."

Casey did take the train back to the depot at Chicago. But that wasn't the end of the trip. He picked up a fireman, and asked the passengers if they wanted to go along to 'Frisco.

"I'm going!" said Uncle Memphis. "If Casey says we'll get there, we will!"

"We may get to 'Frisco but we'll all be dead!" howled Bolsun. "There's a bridge out."

"Casey will get us there, bridge or no bridge," said the Joneses.

Most of the passengers boarded the train again.

"Coming along, Bolsun?" asked Casey.

"I'm a fool to do it," answered Bolsun, "but I will. The Browns are just as brave as the Joneses."

Casey told Bolsun to ride with him in the cab. Then he told the fireman to jingle the brass. He blew a blast on the whistle, opened the throttle, and pulled out. And No. 638 went rolling along, rolling along. Her piston rods shot in and out. She left a long line of smoke against the sky, and she made a noise like thunder.

"Watch those drivers roll!" said Casey. "Watch her steam gauge rise!"

"We'll never get to 'Frisco," said Bolsun. "And if we do, we'll all be dead."

"Build up that fire, tar pot," said Casey to the fireman.

"I'm building her," said the fireman. "I'm putting black on white."

"Go to it, diamond pusher!" said Casey. "I'm going to get to 'Frisco, but I'll need steam!"

No. 638 went highballing along with a terrible roar. Her flags and bunting streamed in the wind. Faster and faster she went, until they got to the valley.

"The bridge is out!" shrieked Bolsun. "It's our last ride!"

Casey glanced at the steam gauge and the water gauge. He opened her throttle wide. No. 638 rushed ahead—and

her speed was so fast she cleared the valley. She flew from one side to the other, and came down with a little bump.

"That's railroading!" said the fireman.

"I can't believe it!" said Bolsun. "I saw it, but I can't believe it!"

After that, of course, Casey didn't have a bit of trouble. He kept No. 638 going, stopping only to pick up coal or water or a fresh fireman. No. 638 passed state after state. She raced up the Rocky Mountains and down again. She crossed plains and valleys and mountains, and by morning she was

in 'Frisco. She'd broken every record ever made.

Casey pulled into the depot, where a crowd of people waited to give him a cheer. Uncle Memphis and the Joneses jumped from the train, laughing and shouting.

"It's a great day for the Joneses!" they said.

"But a bad day for the Browns," said Bolsun. He turned to Casey and said, "Well, Casey, you got her to 'Frisco. You're a great engineer, and now you're Superintendent of the railroad. I hope you like your new job. Good-by, Casey."

"Hold on there, Bolsun," said Casey. "I was meant to be an engineer. You were meant to be a Superintendent. You keep running the railroad, and I'll keep running locomotives.

Only don't tell me to stop playing baseball. This railroad needs Browns *and* Joneses to run her right."

"Casey," said Bolsun, "do you mean that?"

Casey nodded his head.

"Then as Superintendent of this railroad," said Bolsun, "I order you to get out there and pitch your razzle-dazzle ball! Because you're a Jones, and nothing can hurt your touch on the throttle."

Casey pitched his razzle-dazzle ball. After that Bolsun, Casey, Uncle Memphis and the Joneses went to the Blue Goose Restaurant. They had Trainmen's Delights all around, with speeches and a general good time.

And ever since then, there have been both Joneses and Browns on the railroad.

HOW
OLD STORMALONG
CAPTURED
MOCHA DICK

STORY BY
IRWIN SHAPIRO

PICTURES BY
DONALD McKAY

THere are many stories about who captured Mocha Dick, the Great White Whale, or Moby Dick, as he was sometimes called. But any sailorman worth his salt knows that it was Old Stormalong—and he had to become a cowboy to do it.

Alfred Bulltop Stormalong was the greatest sailor who ever lived. He stood four fathoms tall in his stocking feet. His eyes were as blue as a calm sea. His hair was as black as a storm cloud. He could whistle shrill like the wind in the rigging; he could hoot like a foghorn; and he could talk ordinary, just like anyone else. Stormalong had one fault. He was always complaining that they didn't make ships big enough for him.

One windy night Stormalong was sitting in the Sailors'

Snug Haven, the inn that served the best shark soup in the town of Nantucket. He was sitting cross-legged on the floor so that his head wouldn't bump the ceiling. He ate six dozen oysters, then called for some shark soup, which he drank from a dory. Beside him sat Captain Joshua Skinner of the good ship *Dolphin*, and some members of the crew. Stormalong was to sail with them the next morning to catch whales in the Pacific Ocean.

"Captain Skinner," said Stormalong, "on this voyage I'm going to capture Mocha Dick."

"Hm," said Captain Skinner. "You've said that five times before. And five times the white whale escaped you."

"This time he won't escape!" shouted Stormalong, hooting like a foghorn. Then he added in an ordinary voice, "And I

mean it, too."

"Hm," said Captain Skinner. "You meant it the other five
times. And still Mocha Dick swims the seas."

"Aye, 'tis easy to capture the white whale—with words,"
said a little sailor with red whiskers, while all the other sailors
laughed.

"Laugh while you may," said Stormalong angrily. "You'll
be singing a different tune when the *Dolphin* comes back
to port."

"If you are so sure of yourself," said the innkeeper, "write
it down here." And he handed Stormalong one of the slates
on which he kept accounts.

"Aye, that I will," said Stormalong. Picking up the slate,
he wrote in big letters:

On this voyage of the Dolphin I will capture Mocha Dick.

Signed, Alfred Bulltop Stormalong

The innkeeper hung the slate up over the fireplace for all to see.

"Aye, mateys!" roared Stormalong. "This time Mocha Dick will meet his doom!"

Stormalong finished his shark soup in one gulp. Then he whistled shrill like the wind in the rigging, and left the inn.

The next morning a crowd of people was at the dock to say good-by to the *Dolphin's* brave crew.

"Good luck, lads!" they shouted. "A short voyage and a greasy one! Fair winds, calm seas! Beware of Mocha Dick!"

63

"Let Mocha Dick beware, for Alfred Bulltop Stormalong is out to capture him!" said Stormalong, hooting like a foghorn.

"Belay there! Enough of your boasting!" said Captain Skinner. Then he turned to the first mate and said, "Cast off!"

And a cheer went up as the *Dolphin* caught the wind in her sails and went out to the open sea.

For nine months the *Dolphin* sailed the Pacific Ocean. Wherever she went, there was always a lookout in the crow's nest high on the mast. Every time the lookout spied a whale, he would shout, "Blo-o-ows! Thar she blows!" And the men would jump into rowboats and give chase to the whale.

One day the lookout in the crow's nest called out,

"*Blo-o-ows!* Thar she blows! Whale off the port side! Thar she blows and breaches! And Mocha Dick, at that!"

"Man the boats!" ordered the captain. "Lower away!"

The men set out over the side of the ship in little boats and rowed toward Mocha Dick. Stormalong stood in the stern of his boat, waving his harpoon in the air.

"After him, me hearties!" he shouted. "Faster, lads, faster! There he is now!"

And indeed they could see Mocha Dick's ugly face rising out of the sea. With a rumble and a roar the Great White Whale sent a spout of water high into the air. He was almost as big as the *Dolphin,* and he was the color of sea-foam in the light of a misty moon. As if to warn Stormalong, he opened his mouth and showed his great sharp teeth.

"After him, mateys!" cried Stormalong. "A dead whale or a stove boat!"

With a shout, Stormalong let his harpoon fly at Mocha Dick. It stuck in the whale's back. But Mocha Dick just gave himself a shake and began to swim away. The harpoon was attached to the boat by a long rope, and as Mocha Dick swam along he pulled the boat after him.

"Hold fast, mates!" said Stormalong. "Here we go on a sleigh ride!"

Swoosh! And off they went across the water. Faster and faster swam Mocha Dick, with the little boat bobbing and bouncing after him. Soon they had left the *Dolphin* far behind.

Suddenly Mocha Dick stopped. He heaved himself into

the air, and the rope broke with a snap. The harpoon remained in his back, a little bit of rope flying from it like a flag of victory. He dove below the water, gave a flip of his tail, and the boat overturned. With a splash, Stormalong and his mates tumbled into the sea.

"We are lost!" cried one of the sailors. "Mocha Dick is coming back! He will swallow us all!"

But Mocha Dick just pushed his way close to Stormalong and opened his mouth in a big grin. His body shook as though he were laughing. Then he spouted a stream of water right into Stormalong's face, grinned again, and swam away.

"By my boots and breeches!" burst out a little sailor with a lot of red whiskers. "Mocha Dick laughed at Stormalong, and laughed at Stormalong, and spit in his eye!"

All the sailors began to laugh so hard that they almost went to the bottom of the sea. They laughed until their sides ached, and then they laughed some more. They were still laughing when the *Dolphin* caught up with them

"What's so funny?" asked Captain Skinner after the men had climbed on board.

"Mocha Dick laughed at Stormalong and spit in his eye!" said the little sailor with red whiskers.

Captain Skinner began to laugh so hard that the first mate had to grab him by the seat of his pants to keep him from falling overboard. Then the second mate had to grab the first mate to keep *him* from falling overboard.

"And Stormalong the man who boasted that he would capture Mocha Dick!" sputtered the captain. "Ho, ho! Ha, ha!"

"Ho, ho! Ha, ha! Har, har!" laughed the sailors. "Ho, har!"
The little sailor with red whiskers began to sing:

"Stormalong said he'd get Mocha Dick,
    Aye, mates, 'tis no lie,
But the Great White Whale just laughed in his face,
    And spit right in his eye.
To my aye, aye, right in Stormalong's eye,
To my aye, aye, Mister Stormalong's eye."

Stormalong felt so ashamed that he went below and didn't
come up on deck for a week.
For three more months the *Dolphin* sailed the Pacific.
Stormalong did his share of the work, but he never hooted like

a foghorn or whistled shrill like the wind in the rigging. He hardly said a word.

When the *Dolphin* slid into the harbor at Nantucket, the sailors told everyone what had happened. Soon all Nantucket knew that Mocha Dick had laughed at Stormalong and spit in his eye. Poor Stormalong ran away to the beach where he could be alone.

All day long he sat on the beach, sighing and sighing. He sighed so hard that the sea became choppy. At last Stormalong picked himself up and walked to the Sailors' Snug Haven.

The first thing he saw when he entered the inn was the slate hanging over the fireplace. And on it were the words:

70

**On this voyage of the Dolphin I will capture
Mocha Dick.**

Signed, Alfred Bulltop Stormalong

Below these words someone had written:

**But the Great White Whale just laughed at him
and spit in his eye.**

Stormalong sat down and ordered some shark soup, which
he drank from a dory. He topped it off with a keg of New
England rum, then went over to Captain Skinner and said,
"Captain, I've made my last voyage."

"Surely not, laddie," said Captain Skinner kindly. "Oh, no!"

"Aye, Captain," said Stormalong. "I'll never go to sea again. I'm going to be a farmer."

"A farmer!" said Captain Skinner. "You'll never be a farmer, my lad. You've got salt water in your veins. Wherever you go, you'll hear the sea calling to you."

"No," said Stormalong. "They don't build ships big enough for me. I can't get the kinks out of my muscles. And if I can't get the kinks out of my muscles, I can't capture Mocha Dick. And if I can't capture Mocha Dick, I'm no whaler. And if I'm no whaler, I'm no sailor. And if I'm no sailor, the sea is no place for me. I'm going off to be a farmer."

"Well, lad," said Captain Skinner, "if you must go, you must. Good luck to you, and may you reach a safe harbor. But you'll be coming back to sea some day. And when you

do, old Captain Joshua Skinner will give you a berth."

"Thank you, Captain," said Stormalong. "Good-by, Captain."

The next morning Stormalong left Nantucket for the mainland. His dufflebag over his shoulder, he walked down the road. In the light of the morning sun his shadow stretched before him, three counties long.

Stormalong rambled about the Hudson Valley, then stepped over the Allegheny Mountains and ambled about the Shenandoah Valley. He took a little side trip to the Cumberland Mountains, and spent a day in the Tennessee Valley. He walked along the Ohio River, then over the rolling hills of Indiana and the prairies of Illinois. But not until he crossed the Mississippi River to Missouri did he find what he was

looking for.

"Aye," said Stormalong, "this is a country where a full-sized man can get the kinks out of his muscles."

He was in a great forest, where men with axes were chopping down trees. Clong! Clong! went the axes, and the trees crashed to the ground.

"Are you farmers, mateys?" asked Stormalong in his foghorn voice. All the men stopped their work to look at him.

"I reckon we are," said one of the men.

"That's good," said Stormalong. "I'm new to farming, and I'll thank you to tell me what to do."

"Right now we're clearing away the forest so's we can grow our crops," was the answer.

Stormalong borrowed the biggest ax they had, then said,

"Now, mates, just sit down in the shade and rest a while. I mean to do some plain and fancy chopping, to get the kinks out of my muscles."

Stormalong rolled up his sleeves and went to work. By nightfall he had cleared enough land for a hundred farms.

"Who are you?" asked the astonished farmers.

"Alfred Bulltop Stormalong is the name, mateys," said Stormalong. "They don't make ships big enough for me, so I can't get the kinks out of my muscles. If I can't get the kinks out of my muscles, I can't capture Mocha Dick. And if I can't capture Mocha Dick, I'm no whaler. And if I'm no whaler, then I'm no sailor. And if I'm no sailor, my place is on shore. So I came out here to be a farmer, and I'll thank you to tell me just what to do, and how to do it."

And he hooted like a foghorn and whistled shrill like the wind in the rigging.

"The next thing is to clear out the stumps and stones and start planting," said the farmers. "But first you'd better build yourself a cabin to live in."

"A cabin it is, me hearties," said Stormalong. By the time the moon came out he had built himself a cabin.

The next morning Stormalong got up before the sun and started to plow. He didn't use a horse. He just pushed the plow along himself, while stones and stumps flew in all directions.

"Where's your horse?" asked the farmers, more astonished than ever. "We never heard tell of plowing without a horse, a mule, or at least a team of oxen." They shook their heads.

"Didn't know you were supposed to have one," said Stormalong. "But no harm done. If you'll just toss these rocks and stumps into a pile, I'll finish this little job of work."

By the time it was evening, Stormalong had plowed enough land for a hundred farms.

"What's next, me hearties?" he asked. "For I've got the kinks out of my muscles and I'm rarin' to go."

"Plant the seed," said the farmers.

When the farmers got up the next morning, they found Stormalong stretched out under a tree.

"Glad you're up," he said. "I've planted all the seed. Nothing to it. What do I do now?"

"Just wait for the crops to start growing," said the farmers. "Unless you have some cows or chickens or pigs to look

after."

"I can't look after cows or chickens or pigs," said Stormalong. "I'm too big for 'em. But I don't like this idea of waiting. I'll get kinks in my muscles."

It was hard for Stormalong to sit around doing nothing. At night he could hear the wind blowing through the trees of the forest. The leaves went hiss, swish, like the sound of the sea. The branches creaked like the rigging of a ship. Stormalong dreamt that he was a sailor again.

In the daytime Stormalong would climb the tallest tree in the forest. He would gaze out over the rolling hills, which looked like the waves of the sea. The tree swayed in the wind, and Stormalong imagined he was in the crow's nest of the *Dolphin,* keeping a sharp lookout for whale the while.

A big cloud floated past in the sky. To Stormalong it looked like Mocha Dick.

"*Blo-o-ows!*" he shouted. "Thar she blows! Whale off the starboard side! Thar she blows and breaches! And Mocha Dick, at that! After him, me hearties! A dead whale or a stove boat!"

Then one day a storm came up. The sky was as black as the bottom of a well. Lightning flashed, thunder roared, while the wind went howling through the forest like a madman.

"Hooray, a storm!" shouted Stormalong to the farmers. "Now I can get the kinks out of my muscles. Avast there, mateys! Storm ahead! All hands on deck!"

All of a sudden one of the farmers stuck his head out of the window of his cabin, and looked at Stormalong.

"What's all the fuss?" he asked.

"Storm!" said Stormalong. "Pipe all hands on deck! What do farmers do in a storm, matey?"

"Let 'er storm," said the farmer. "Nothing else to do."

Stormalong was so surprised he couldn't say anything. He just stood there, the lightning flashing around his head, the rain dripping down his shoulders.

"I've had enough of this," he said at last. "I can't sit around and do nothing when there's a storm. I guess I just wasn't cut out to be a farmer."

He went to his cabin, threw his dufflebag over his shoulder, then waved good-by to the farmers.

"So long," he said. "I'm going west to be a cowboy."

Stormalong rambled about the dusty plains of Texas, then

ambled over to Oklahoma. He took a side trip to the Rocky Mountains, and followed the Sweetwater River into Wyoming. He walked across the salt flats of Utah and the plateau of Arizona, but not until he came to New Mexico did he find what he was looking for.

"Aye," he said, "this is a country where a full-sized man can get the kinks out of his muscles."

Stormalong went into a store to buy himself a cowboy outfit.

"Matey," he said to the storekeeper, "I want a ten-gallon hat, chaps, a checkered shirt, Spanish boots with pointed toes, silver spurs, and a pretty bandana."

The storekeeper looked Stormalong up and down.

"Stranger," he said, "you're the biggest galoot that ever

blew into this man's town. I can sell you what you want, but it will have to be made special."

It took eight weeks to make Stormalong's cowboy outfit While he was waiting, Stormalong learned how to use a lariat. With his lariat Stormalong lassoed the wild mustang that roamed the plains. The mustang was a little too small for Stormalong, but it was the biggest horse he could get.

Then Stormalong got a job as a cowboy on the Triple Star Ranch.

"Mateys," he said, "I've never been a cowboy before, and I'll thank you to tell me what to do."

"It's round-up time, pardner," said the cowboys. "First thing to do is round up the steers."

"Just sit down and rest yourself, me hearties," said Storm-

along. "I'll round 'em up, just to get the kinks out of my muscles."

When evening came, Stormalong had rounded up all the steers.

"Who are you?" asked the astonished cowboys.

"Alfred Bulltop Stormalong is the name," answered Stormalong. "They don't make ships big enough for me, so I can't get the kinks out of my muscles. If I can't get the kinks out of my muscles, I can't capture Mocha Dick. And if I can't capture Mocha Dick, I'm no whaler. And if I'm no whaler, then I'm no sailor. And if I'm no sailor, my place is on shore. I tried to be a farmer, but I couldn't. So I came out here to be a cowboy, and I'll thank you to tell me what to do."

"The next thing to do is brand the steers," said the cow-

boys.

Stormalong got up before the sun the next morning and started to brand the steers. By the time the cowboys got up all the steers had been branded.

"What's next, me hearties?" asked Stormalong. "For I've got the kinks out of my muscles and I'm rarin' to go."

"Just ride around and keep an eye on the steers. We call it riding herd," said the cowboys.

Stormalong rode herd with the other cowboys. At night they sat around the campfire, playing the guitar and singing songs. Stormalong had a guitar made special, and when he played it the mountains would echo for miles around.

Stormalong soon began to get tired of being a cowboy. There wasn't enough to do, and he was getting kinks in his

muscles. At night he would wake up and look around. In the moonlight the plain stretched out like a calm sea, while the mountains stood up like islands.

"Avast, mateys!" shouted Stormalong. "We're becalmed! More sail, more sail! Break out more sail, me hearties, for we must capture Mocha Dick, the Great White Whale!"

One day a huge black cloud filled the sky and the rain began to come down. Lightning flashed, thunder boomed, and the wind raced across the plain like wild horses.

Stormalong waved his ten-gallon hat in the air and shouted, "All hands on deck! Storm blowing up! All hands on deck!" And he hooted like a foghorn and whistled shrill like the wind in the rigging.

"What's the rumpus, pardner?" asked one of the cowboys.

"Storm!" said Stormalong. "What do cowboys do in a storm, matey? She's a-rippin' and a-snortin'."

"Let 'er rip and snort," said the cowboy. "Nothing else to do about it."

Stormalong sat down on a big rock. The wind howled around him, and the water dripped off his hat like a waterfall.

"I just can't sit around and do nothing when there's a storm," he said. "I guess I'm no more a cowboy than I was a farmer."

Stormalong seemed to hear the voice of Captain Skinner saying, "Aye, lad, you'll never be able to give up the sea. You've got salt water in your veins. Wherever you go, you'll hear the sea calling to you."

"You were right, Captain Skinner!" shouted Stormalong.

"Maybe the ships are too small for a full-sized man. Maybe I'll get kinks in my muscles and won't be able to capture Mocha Dick. Maybe I'm no whaler, and maybe I'm no sailor. But I'll go back to sea if I have to be a cabin boy, for I'll never be happy anywhere else."

Stormalong turned his mustang loose on the plains. He threw his dufflebag over one shoulder, and slung his guitar over the other.

"So long, mateys," he said to the cowboys. Then he started walking east, toward Nantucket and the sea.

It was a wet, misty morning when Stormalong got to Nantucket. For a long time he stood on a hill, sniffing in the salt sea air. He could see the harbor, with masts of ships sticking up into the sky. When he caught sight of the waves breaking

on the shore, he hooted like a foghorn and whistled shrill like the wind in the rigging.

"The sea is the place for me," he said. "And now for the Sailors' Snug Haven and some of that good shark soup."

When Stormalong got to the Sailors' Snug Haven he wiped the mist from his eyes and looked around. Everything was the same as it had been. Over the fireplace hung the slate with these words on it:

On this voyage of the Dolphin I will capture Mocha Dick.

Signed, Alfred Bulltop Stormalong

But the Great White Whale just laughed at him and spit in his eye.

"A cowboy in Nantucket!" said a voice behind him. "You're a long way from home, matey."

Stormalong turned around. There sat Captain Skinner.

"The sea is my home, Captain," said Stormalong, hooting like a foghorn and whistling shrill like the wind in the rigging.

"By my boots and breeches!" said the captain. "It's Stormalong, for there's no one else who can hoot like a foghorn and whistle shrill like the wind in the rigging."

"Aye," said Stormalong, "Alfred Bulltop Stormalong it is, and I'll never leave the sea again."

"I knew you'd be back, lad," said Captain Skinner. "Now sit down beside me and tell me your adventures."

Stormalong ordered some shark soup, which he drank from a dory. He told Captain Skinner all his adventures, and when

he had finished he said, "And now, Captain, will you give me
my old berth on the *Dolphin?*"

"Aye, laddie. But you used to complain that the *Dolphin*
was too small for you. Well, she's still the same size, but
you're bigger than ever."

"She'll be big enough for me," said Stormalong. "I'll go to
sea in a washtub if I can't get anything else."

"Spoken like a true seaman!" laughed Captain Skinner.
"Well, I must leave you now, for I've some business to do.
We sail at six tomorrow morning. Be sure that you're on
time."

When Captain Skinner stood up Stormalong saw that one
of his legs was gone. In its place was a wooden peg-leg.

"Your leg, Captain!" said Stormalong. "What happened?"

"It was bit off by Mocha Dick on my last voyage. The

white whale bit off my leg and sent two of my crew to the bottom of the sea."

"Captain Skinner," cried Stormalong, "I won't rest until I've captured Mocha Dick."

"No, lad," said the captain. "Never again will I battle Mocha Dick. He's more fearful than ever. I'll lose no more of my men to the monster." And with that he left the inn.

When Stormalong came on board the *Dolphin* the next morning, the crew began to laugh. He was still wearing his cowboy outfit, and he was so bowlegged from riding the mustang that a ship could have sailed between his legs.

"Avast there, Stormalong!" said Captain Skinner. "Get below and put on some proper duds. Stormalong or no Stormalong, I'll have no cowboys on my ship."

"Captain, I'd like to do as you say, but this cowboy outfit

was made special, and I'm going to keep on wearing it."

Captain Skinner grew red in the face.

"I'm captain of this ship, and you'll obey my orders!" he roared.

"Captain," said Stormalong, "I know you're the captain. But captain or no captain, I'm going to wear my cowboy outfit."

Stormalong began to hop up and down, so that the *Dolphin* rocked in the water.

"Belay there, Stormalong!" shouted the sailors. "Sit down, you're rocking the boat!"

"Stop, Stormalong! You'll sink the ship!" cried the captain.

Stormalong kept hopping up and down.

"I won't stop until you say it's all right for me to wear my cowboy outfit," he said. "And you can lay to that!"

"Wear what you like, you stubborn walrus!" said the captain, and Stormalong stopped hopping up and down.

A crowd had gathered on shore to say good-by to Captain Skinner and his crew.

"Good luck!" they called. "A short voyage and a greasy one!"

Captain Skinner was so angry that he didn't want to say good-by to anyone.

"Cast off!" he bellowed.

The *Dolphin* was raring to go. She took the wind in her sails and made for the open sea.

It was not long before the lookout in the crow's nest sang out, "*Blo-o-ows! Thar she blows! Whale off the port side!*"

"Yipee!" shouted Stormalong, like a cowboy. Still dressed in his cowboy outfit, he jumped into his boat. It made Cap-

tain Skinner angry to see a cowboy in a whaling boat. But he didn't say anything. He was afraid Stormalong would start hopping up and down again.

Stormalong soon showed that he could still catch whales.

"By the Great Horn Spoon," said Captain Skinner to himself, "Stormalong is a real sailorman, even if he does dress like a cowboy."

Then one day the lookout in the crow's nest shouted, "*Blo-o-ows!* Thar she blows and breaches! And Mocha Dick, at that! It's the Great White Whale, mates!"

"All hands aloft!" ordered Captain Skinner. "Break out more sail. We're going to get away from these waters as fast as we can. I'll not battle Mocha Dick again."

"Captain," said Stormalong, "are you really going to let it be said that a Nantucket whaler ran away from a whale?"

"Mocha Dick is no ordinary whale. He is a monster, and I'll lose no more of my men to him," said Captain Skinner.

"Let me go after him," begged Stormalong. "He'll not laugh at me this time."

"Stow your chatter and help loose the sails," Captain Skinner bellowed. "I'm the captain of the *Dolphin*, Mr. Stormalong, and I forbid you to go after Mocha Dick. Now get aloft before I have you put in irons!"

But just then the lookout in the crow's nest gave a terrible cry.

"Mocha Dick is coming after us! He's going to bump the ship!"

Captain Skinner ran to the rail. There was Mocha Dick, roaring and snorting and plunging. He rushed straight at the *Dolphin*, and *bump!* the stern of the ship rose into the air.

"We are lost!" cried the sailors. "Mocha Dick will sink the ship. We are lost!"

"Not yet, mateys!" said Stormalong.

And leaping over the rail, he landed smack on Mocha Dick's back.

"Yipee!" shouted Stormalong, and he began to ride Mocha Dick like a cowboy riding a bucking broncho. He hung on with one hand and waved his ten-gallon hat with the other.

Mocha Dick thrashed about, trying to throw Stormalong off his back. Stormalong only laughed and waved his hat again.

"Ride him, cowboy!" cheered the sailors. "Ride him, Stormalong!"

Snorting with rage, the white whale leaped into the air. Then he dove deep under the water, trying to drown Storm-

along. But Stormalong took a deep breath and held his nose. Mocha Dick heaved himself into the air again. He tossed and twisted and turned. Then he began to swim furiously about. He went zig-zagging across the ocean so fast that the zigs and the zags became all mixed up. Captain Skinner and his crew grew dizzy watching them.

"Ride him, cowboy!" they yelled. "Ride him, Stormalong!"

"Yipee! *Wahoo!*" shouted Stormalong, hooting like a foghorn and whistling shrill like the wind in the rigging.

For three days Stormalong rode Mocha Dick. Once when he passed close to the ship he called out, "I'm getting hungry, mates. How about some coffee and a sandwich?"

The cook made him a washtub full of coffee and a sandwich three yards long. When Stormalong passed by again, a sailor stood on the jib boom and handed them to Storm-

along.

On the third day Mocha Dick's strength was almost gone. But he made one great try to throw Stormalong off his back. He dove deep under the water. He turned somersaults. He tossed and twisted and rolled from side to side. He went around in circles, like a dog chasing his tail. Around and around he went, until the water foamed like milk. He leaped high into the air and came down with a tremendous splash. Then a shudder ran through his body and he was still.

"Hooray!" shouted the sailors. "Hooray for Stormalong!"

"This is the end of the Great White Whale," said a big sailor with a crooked nose. "He just wore himself out."

"No," said a little sailor with red whiskers, "he died of a broken heart."

"Hooray!" shouted the sailors again and again. "Hooray

for Stormalong!"

"Aye, lads, you may well cheer," said Captain Skinner. "Stormalong has done a great thing. No more will Mocha Dick send honest seamen to their death."

Then the *Dolphin* dropped anchor beside the huge body of the white whale. The sailors cut him up and boiled the blubber for the sperm oil. In a few days the job was done, and they set sail for Nantucket.

"We're loaded to the hatches with oil. We'll all be rich," said Captain Skinner. He felt so happy that he danced a hornpipe across the deck. Tappy, tappy, tap, went his peg-leg.

Stormalong sat down on a hatch and rested his feet on the jib boom. He picked up his guitar and began to sing loud and gay.

"Twang, twang! Plunk, plunk! Plunkety, twang!" went the

guitar. The deep notes sounded like a pipe organ and the high notes were as sweet as violins. Stormalong sang *Home on the Range* and *Bury Me Not on the Lone Prairie.*

The crew came back with *Blow the Man Down.* Stormalong topped them with *As I Was Walking Down the Streets of Laredo.* Then they all chimed in with *Whiskey for My Johnnie.*

The sound of their ·music was so sweet that all the fish lifted their heads out of the water to listen. Sea gulls flew after the ship, beating their wings in time to the music. All the way across the ocean the fish followed the *Dolphin.* In schools and shoals and droves they came, and the New England fishermen caught the greatest catch of seafish that was ever caught in all history.

When the *Dolphin* got into Nantucket, the crew was

singing, each man-jack louder than the next:

"Then give me a whaleman, wherever he be,
Who fears not a fish that can swim the salt sea;
Then give me a tight ship, and under snug sail,
And last lay me 'side the noble sperm whale;
In the Indian Ocean,
Or Pacific Ocean,
No matter *what* ocean;
Pull ahead, yo heave O!"

When the crowd at the dock heard about Mocha Dick they gave such a shout that the clouds scattered clear out of the sky.

Stormalong waved to the crowd, and hurried to the Sailors' Snug Haven. He picked up the slate, on which were the words:

On this voyage of the Dolphin I will capture Mocha Dick.

Signed, Alfred Bulltop Stormalong

But the Great White Whale just laughed at him and spit in his eye.

"No more he doesn't!" shouted Stormalong. He smashed the slate into a thousand pieces. "Mateys," he roared, "I captured Mocha Dick. If I captured Mocha Dick, I'm a whaler. And if I'm a whaler, then I'm a sailor. And if I'm a sailor, my place is on the sea. And the sea is no place for a cowboy. I'll never wear my cowboy outfit again, even though it was made special. And you can lay to that!"

Then Stormalong sat down and ate twelve dozen oysters,

fifty-two codfish balls, sixty-seven lobsters, ten pounds of whale steak, a dory full of shark soup, and another full of clam chowder. For dessert he had a New England boiled dinner, three or four apple pies, and a nibble or two of maple-sugar candy. He washed it all down with a keg of New England rum, then hooted like a foghorn and whistled shrill like the wind in the rigging.

"Hooray for Old Stormalong!" shouted all the crew. "Hooray, hooray, *hooray!*"

After staying on shore for a week, Stormalong sailed off again on the *Dolphin*. He made many voyages in many ships, until Donald McKay built a ship called the *Courser*. She was so big that the captain and his officers had to ride around on horseback. The mast was so tall that it had to be bent back on hinges to let the sun and the moon go past.

When Stormalong saw the *Courser* he said, "There's my ship," and asked the captain for a berth.

But that's another story.

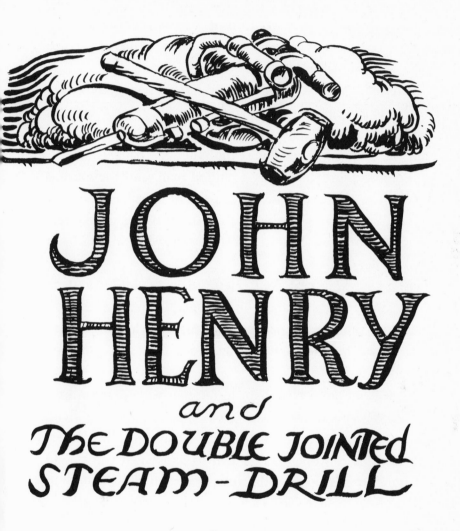

JOHN HENRY
and
THE DOUBLE JOINTED STEAM-DRILL

By

IRWIN SHAPIRO

WITH DRAWINGS BY JAMES DAUGHERTY

FOR a long time now there's been talk about John Henry. For a long time now there have been songs about John Henry. Talk and songs alike say he died with his hammer in his hand. Yes, beat the double-jointed steam drill, then died with his hammer in his hand.

No such thing! Couldn't any steam drill send John Henry to his lonely grave! No, sir! Not John Henry! He did feel poorly for a while, and weary and blue. But in the end he ran the steam drill right into the ground. That's a fact.

Because John Henry was a natural man, and the greatest steel driver that ever was. He was almost as tall as a box car is long. His arms were thicker than the cross-ties on the rail-road. His skin was black, and it glistened like a brand-new pair of ten-dollar shoes.

My, my, how that John Henry man could drive steel! Why, each time he raised his hammer, it made a rainbow round his shoulder. And when he brought his hammer down, folks three hundred miles away heard an awful rumbling sound.

How come John Henry got to messing with a steam drill? Well, you might say it was on account of the Big Bend Tunnel. Or you might say it was on account of John Hardy. Then again you might say it had to happen—it was bound to be. Any which way, the fuss began on the night John Henry first came to New Orleans.

That night John Henry walked along, wearing his overalls and his clodhopper shoes. He meant to see the sights, and he did. First he had him a look at the houses with their little iron-railed balconies. Then he headed for the levee to cast his eyes over the steamboats. He hadn't gone very far, though, before he stopped.

"I declare," said John Henry. "I do declare."

The streets were just jam-packed full of folks. They all

106

had masks over their faces. They were dressed up as pirates
and devils and clowns and what-all.

John Henry stooped low and asked a clown, "Is it always
like this in New Orleans?"

"Ha! ha!" laughed the clown, thumping him with a stocking filled with flour. "As if you didn't know the Mardi Gras Carnival was going on!"

John Henry had never seen a town before, let alone a Mardi Gras Carnival. While he was trying to puzzle it out, the clown tugged at his sleeve.

"That's a fine get-up you have," said the clown. "But we'd better hurry or we'll be late. Come on!"

Shaking his head, John Henry followed the clown around a corner. A parade was coming down the street, led by the King of the Carnival on his golden throne. Behind the King were men carrying torches, and floats of dragons and giants. Bands blew music. The folks cheered and threw confetti over each other.

"Great day in the morning!" said John Henry.

And the next thing that happened, he was marching in the parade.

Anything John Henry did, he made up a song to go with it. Now he started to strut and sing:

> Mardi Gras!
> Don't know what it means!
> But it's fine to be here
> In New Orleans!

The parade wound around town until it came to a big ballroom. The folks rushed inside, pushing John Henry in, too. He danced like the rest, tossing off a buck-and-wing that had the folks yelling for more. He was just beginning a new step when the clock struck twelve.

"Time to unmask!" shouted the King of the Carnival.

All the folks took off their masks. That is, all except John Henry.

"You there!" said the King. "Twelve o'clock! Time to unmask!"

"S'cuse me, King," said John Henry. "I ain't got no mask."

109

"Then wipe that lampblack off! And take off your stilts, so we'll know who you are!"

"That's no lampblack, King," said John Henry. "And I'm not wearing any stilts, neither."

"You mean to tell me you're just naturally that way?" said the King.

"Yes, suh," answered John Henry. "I'm nothin' but a natural man."

The King reared back on his throne.

"Where you from, boy!" he roared. "What are you doing here?"

There wasn't another sound in the whole ballroom. The band had stopped playing. The folks had stopped dancing. Everybody was standing around, watching John Henry.

And John Henry said, "I'm from the Black River Country where the sun don't ever shine. I've picked the cotton till I could pick cotton in my sleep. I got an itch in my heel, so I traveled down to New Orleans to get me a job of work."

"Throw him out!" said the folks. "Put him in the chain gang! He's too uppety for his own good! Send him to the chain gang!"

"Just a minute!" said the King, holding up his hand. He turned to John Henry and said, "Look here, boy! You claim you're a country boy and came here to do a job of work. Think you could roust cotton?"

"Think I could, King," answered John Henry.

"All right," said the King. "Everybody out to the levee! Send for John Hardy and tell him to be at my steamboat! We're going to have some fun!"

As soon as they heard that, the folks streamed out of the ballroom. They piled into carriages, lighting torches so they could see what was going on. With John Henry walking beside them, they rode to the levee.

"Halt!" ordered the King when they reached the steamboat. He stood up in his carriage and called out, "John Hardy! John Hardy!"

"Comin', cap'n," said John Hardy, stepping out from the crowd.

This John Hardy was a big man, though not as big as John Henry. He was built a lot closer to the ground.

He had a voice like a bullfrog, and was dressed mighty fancy for a rouster. He wore a checked shirt, blue jeans, and a belt studded with rhinestones.

"This boy thinks he can roust cotton," said the King.

"Do tell," said John Hardy, giving the folks a wink. "Country boy, ain't he?"

John Hardy looked John Henry up and down.

He said, "Mmm. He got the heft, all right. He got the size. But it takes a man to roust this old cotton."

"That's me, then," said John Henry. " 'Cause I'm a natural man."

"Takes a man by the name o' John to roust cotton," said John Hardy.

"That's me again," said John Henry. " 'Cause my name is John Henry, and I'm proud of it."

"Huh!" said John Hardy. " 'Tain't you a-tall. It's me. I'm John Hardy, and I'm the best rouster on this here river."

Just then a pretty girl in a red dress spoke up.

"Don't pay him no mind, John Henry!" she said.

"You keep out of this, Pollie Ann," said John Hardy.

"Hush your big mouth," said Pollie Ann. "John Henry can roust cotton if he wants."

John Hardy threw back his head and laughed.

"Wantin' ain't doin'," he said. "And if I don't roust this country boy off his feet, I'll never hold a hook in my hand again!"

"Well, go to it!" said the King. "That's what we're waiting to see."

John Hardy nodded his head. He gave John Henry a rousting hook, and the two of them began to roust cotton. John

Henry rolled his bale to the gangplank and began to cross it.

"Roll that cotton, John Henry!" said Pollie Ann. "Roll it good!"

But as soon as John Henry set foot on the gangplank, it began to buck and spring. John Henry tromped down hard, and the plank sprang right back. John Henry tromped down even harder. The plank arched up high, heaving him head over heels into the air. And John Henry fell into the river with a mighty splash.

"Look at that country boy!" laughed the folks.

"What did I tell you!" said John Hardy.

But Pollie Ann called out, "Try again, John Henry! First time's the hardest!"

John Henry crawled out of the river, dripping wet. He walked up to the gangplank, put one foot on it, and tested its spring. Swaying back and forth, he sang:

> *Roust that cotton*
> *But don't be a fool,*
> *'Cause this gangplank kick*
> *Like grandpa's mule.*
> *Roust that cotton,*
> *Roust that cotton, oh!*

Then John Henry rolled his bale, and this time he rolled it right. He strutted across the plank, rolling two bales to John Hardy's one.

"Look out, John Hardy!" said the folks. "Might be that John Henry can really roust!"

"Huh!" said John Hardy. "Let him try this."

Sinking his hook into a bale, he raised it to his shoulder. And he toted that bale faster than John Henry could roll. Halfway across the plank, though, his knees started to sag.

"Guess you need a little help," said John Henry.

He hoisted his own bale to his left shoulder. Then he put his hook under John Hardy's belt. He picked him up, bale and all, and hoisted him to his right shoulder. He cake-walked across the gangplank and dropped his load on the steamboat deck.

The folks laughed fit to bust. The King almost fell out of his carriage. Pollie Ann jumped up and down. As for John Hardy—well, he was just full of shame. He threw down his hook and ran off.

"No need to do that!" said John Henry. "There's room on this river for two good rousters!"

"Let him go," said the King. "Because you're a natural man and the best rouster I ever saw. You can stay in New Orleans, son, and work for me. You be here tomorrow morning, ready to roll that cotton."

"I'll be ready, King," said John Henry.

"He sure enough will," said Pollie Ann. "Because I'm going to fix him a snack to keep up his strength."

And while the folks went back to the ballroom, John Henry walked off with Pollie Ann.

After that John Henry rousted cotton every day. When he was through working, Pollie Ann would make him a snack of hog jowls, chittlin's, cracklin's, corn pone, side meat, and greens. John Henry liked Pollie Ann's cooking and he liked Pollie Ann. It wasn't long before they were married. They rented them a little house with a piano in it and settled down. Everything went along just fine, and it looked like John Henry would keep on rousting cotton till nobody knows when.

Then one night John Henry and Pollie Ann were in their house, sitting at the piano. While Pollie Ann tickled the ivories, John Henry sang. All of a sudden they heard a knocking at the door.

"Who's that?" called John Henry.

"Nobody else but me," said a bullfrog voice. And who should come walking in but John Hardy. He had on a brown box coat, a pearl-gray hat, and ox-blood shoes. He puffed away at a cheroot, and he said, "Evenin', Brother Henry!

Evenin', Miss Pollie!"

"Well, I declare," said John Henry. "I do declare. I'm sure enough glad to see you, John Hardy. And I'm sure glad you got no hard feelings. 'Cause I never did mean to roust you off the river."

John Hardy flicked some ash off his cheroot.

"Maybe so, maybe so," he said. "Of course roustin' is all right for a country boy. I was aimin' to leave the river anyway."

"Where you at now, John Hardy? What are you doin'?" asked John Henry.

"I'm drivin' steel on the railroad," said John Hardy. "I goes here, and I goes there—wherever they're layin' track."

"Drivin' steel," said John Henry slowly. "Sounds right nice."

"Glad to hear you say so," said John Hardy. Then he stepped close to John Henry and shouted, "'Cause I ain't forgot how you shamed me in front of the folks! And should you care to drive steel against me—well, there's a job in

Alabama right now. That's where I'll be."

And he walked out, slamming the door behind him.

"Drivin' steel," said John Henry, his eyes shining.

"You don't have to go," said Pollie Ann. "You doin' all right roustin' the cotton."

John Henry played a chord on the piano and sang:

> I can pick the cotton, and I can roust it, too,
> Yes, pick the cotton, and I can roust it, too,
> But drivin' steel is what I'd like to do.

"Then stop your moonin' around," said Pollie Ann. "You make yourself a pack of clothes and go."

That's just what John Henry did. He said good-by to Pollie Ann and set off for Alabama. When he got to the place where the railroad was laying track, work had already started. A crew of men was driving steel, and with them was John Hardy.

"Well, Long John," said John Hardy to John Henry, "so you think you can drive steel."

"Well, Short John," said John Henry, "it looks like a job for a natural man. And that's me."

"Huh!" said John Hardy, making believe he was trying to hide a laugh. He took John Henry to the foreman and he said, "Cap'n, here's a man thinks he can drive steel. But big as he is, I'm goin' to burn him out in no time."

"I don't care about burning anybody out," said the cap'n. "I just want to see those spikes in those rails. Your friend looks like he can handle a hammer, so go ahead."

John Hardy and John Henry each picked them up a nine-pound hammer.

And John Hardy roared, "Cap'n, give me a whole line of spike holders! Let 'em stand in a row and look out—'cause I'm goin' to drive on down and mash those spikes in fast!"

John Henry said quietly, "Cap'n, you just give me one spike

holder. That will be enough for me."

The cap'n gave the word to the spike holders, and a dozen of them lined up on one side of the track. John Hardy began driving in the spikes, and he went right down the line.

John Henry's one spike holder knelt at his feet. John Henry took a few practice swings with his hammer, then began to drive steel. After a little while he sang:

> This old hammer
> Ring like silver,
> Shine like gold, boys,
> Shine like gold.

And every time he raised his hammer, it made a rainbow round his shoulder. And when he brought his hammer down, it made an awful rumbling sound.

All the same, John Hardy was way ahead of John Henry. He went on mashing down the spikes, his arms pumping away.

"Hey, country boy!" he said. "Ain't you burned out yet? You sings pretty, but singin' ain't swingin', and that's what drives in this steel."

John Henry smiled and said to the cap'n, "Cap'n, I don't need any spike holder a-tall. You can put my holder to holdin' spikes for John Hardy."

"You're crazy, boy!" said the cap'n. "Nobody can drive steel without a holder."

John Henry just smiled. He put a handful of spikes in his mouth, the way a tailor does pins. He picked up two nine-pound hammers. Then leaning over the track, he spit out the spikes, one by one. And he drove in each spike with a couple of taps of his two hammers. It wasn't long before he'd left John Hardy far behind.

"Look at him go!" said all the steel drivers and spike holders. "That *is* a natural man! John Henry is a steel-drivin' man if there ever was one!"

119

As for John Hardy—well, he was full of shame. He threw down his hammer and ran off.

After that John Henry drove steel every day. He traveled
to almost every state of the Union, driving steel. He worked

for the B. & O. Railroad, and the C. & O. Railroad. He worked
for the Houston and Texas Central, the St. Louis Western,
the Mississippi, Kansas and Texas, and lots more. Wherever
he went, he sent for Pollie Ann. They'd live in a tent, and
Pollie Ann would fix him snacks of hog jowls, chittlin's,
cracklin's, corn pone, side meat, and greens. Everything went
along fine, and it looked like he'd drive steel on the railroad
till nobody knows when.

Then one day John Henry came walking into the tent and
said to Pollie Ann, "The C. & O. Railroad is buildin' the Big
Bend Tunnel in West Virginia."

"That's nice," said Pollie Ann.

"They'll be needin' men to drive steel," said John Henry.
Pollie Ann didn't say anything, so John Henry went on.

"It ain't like drivin' steel on the railroad," he said. "No,
suh. You got to push that ol' mountain down."

122

Pollie Ann whirled around.

"John Henry," she said, "has that no-'count John Hardy been here? Is that it?"

"Why, no! No, ma'am! I just heard the news is all," said John Henry.

"John Henry," said Pollie Ann, "you don't have to go. You doin' all right drivin' steel on the railroad."

John Henry hung his head. Pollie Ann gave him a long look, then said, "Well, don't stand here moonin' like a sick cow. You got your mind set on goin', so get along."

And John Henry did. He got together a little pack of clothes, and set out, singing:

> *I'm a natural man, and I got to get around,*
> *I'm a natural man, and I got to get around,*
> *So good-by, Pollie, 'cause I'm West Virginia bound.*

By the time John Henry reached West Virginia, the work had already started. The steel drivers were up on the mountain, driving steel. The turners and shakers were turning and shaking. The blacksmiths were putting new points on the jumpers. Walking among them all was the foreman, Cap'n Tommy Walters.

John Henry's shadow fell over the mountain, and everybody looked up.

"Great Gadfrey!" said Cap'n Walters. "Who are you, boy? Look like a regular giant."

"No, suh, cap'n," said John Henry. "I ain't no giant. I'm nothin' but a man, a natural man. I've been drivin' steel on the railroad, and now I'd like to do the same for you."

"Well, maybe," said Cap'n Walters. "But building a tunnel isn't like laying track. You've got to drive the steel jumper right into the mountain. You've got to drive her deep, so's we can put dynamite in the hole and blast out a tunnel. And she's a hard rock mountain, solid clear through."

"Suits me, cap'n," said John Henry.

"Well, you can try it," said Cap'n Walters. "You can have Li'l Willie there for a turner and shaker."

John Henry put down his pack of clothes and whipped off his shirt. He rubbed a little rock dust on his hands, and a little more on the handle of his hammer. He waited a minute while Li'l Willie knelt at his feet holding the jumper. Then he raised his hammer and began to sing. At the end of every line he sang, he brought his hammer down. It went like this:

> *There ain't no hammer*—clong!
> *Upon this mountain*—clang!
> *Ring like mine, boys*—bong!
> *Ring like mine*—whang!
> *This ol' hammer*—bom!
> *Ring like silver*—bam!
> *Shine like gold, boys*—whom!
> *Shine like gold*—wham!

And every time John Henry raised his hammer, it made a rainbow round his shoulder. And when he brought his hammer down, it made an awful rumbling sound.

"Look at that John Henry, cap'n!" said all the men. "Look at him whop that steel!"

They sang back at John Henry:

> *If I could hammer*
> *Like John Henry,*
> *If I could hammer*
> *Like John Henry,*
> *Lawd, I'd be a man,*
> *Lawd, I'd be a man.*

After that John Henry drove steel on the mountain every day. He sent for Pollie Ann, and they rented them a little house with a piano in it. When John Henry was through working, Pollie Ann would fix him a snack of hog jowls, chitlin's, cracklin's, corn pone, side meat, and greens. Everything went along fine, and it looked like John Henry would keep driving steel on the mountain till nobody knows when.

Then one day John Henry was hammering away, hammering away. The drivers alongside him were doing the same, and Cap'n Walters was saying:

"Come on, you bullies! Drive that steel! We've got to build the Big Bend Tunnel to let the trains run through!"

All of a sudden they heard a noise—chug-chug, chug-chug!

"Sound like the train comin' already," laughed John Henry. "Even before we got the track laid."

And chuggety-chug, chug-chug, something came scooting around the bend of the mountain. This little old something had a smokestack and wheels, and yet it wasn't a locomotive. It hissed and puffed steam, and yet it wasn't exactly a steam engine. Two men were riding on it. One of them was wearing a ten-gallon hat and a blue serge suit. The other had on a checked shirt, blue jeans, and a belt studded with rhinestones.

"Hello, Big Stuff!" he said in a bullfrog voice.

"I declare!" said John Henry. "I do declare! If it ain't John Hardy! Howdy, Small Stuff!"

"It's me, all right, Long John," said John Hardy.

"What's that you're sittin' on, Short John?" asked John Henry.

"A steam drill, Brother Henry—a steam drill," answered John Hardy. "She's new-fangled! She's triple-plated! And she's double-jointed! Yes, suh!"

"Sure enough?" said John Henry. "But what does she do?"

John Hardy opened his mouth to tell him, but the man in the ten-gallon hat jumped off.

"I'll take care of this," he said. He grabbed Cap'n Walters' hand and shook it. "Pleased to meet you, Mr. Walters. Just call me Breezy Sam. Ain't she pretty?"

"Well . . ." said Cap'n Walters.

"Glad you agree," said Breezy Sam. "Knew you would, though. This here double-jointed steam drill is the wonder of the age. She drills holes in the rock faster than any ten men can drive steel. And it only takes one man to handle her. Cap'n, two-three of these steam drills will get your tunnel through in no time."

John Henry stooped low to have a good look at the steam drill. John Hardy pulled a lever and blew steam in his face.

"Look out, boy!" shouted John Hardy. "She'll chew your head off if you ain't careful! I'm holdin' her back, but it ain't easy. So stand back before I drill this mountain out from under your feet."

John Henry looked at Cap'n Walters and the two of them let out a laugh.

The cap'n said to Breezy Sam, "You'd better peddle your contraption somewhere else, mister. As long as John Henry is driving steel for me, I don't need any steam drill."

"Huh!" said John Hardy. "Just let me run this little ol' steam drill against John Henry! Let me show him, Mr. Sam!"

"Why, can't any man stand up against the steam drill. Can't any man beat a machine," said Breezy Sam.

"How about it, John Henry?" asked Cap'n Walters.

"Cap'n," said John Henry, "a man ain't nothin' but a man, even if he is a natural man. But before I let that steam drill run me down, I'll die with my hammer in my hand."

"What do you say to a match?" said the cap'n to Breezy Sam.

They talked it over, and decided to hold a match the next day. The steam drill against John Henry, and the one that drove the deepest hole would win. If John Henry lost, the cap'n promised to buy some steam drills. If the steam drill lost, Breezy Sam would pay Cap'n Walters five hundred dollars.

"Well, tall boy," said John Hardy, "this is the time you ain't goin' to shame me before the folks."

"Well, small boy," said John Henry, "we'll see about that."

"We sure will, tall fry," said John Hardy.

"We sure enough will, small fry," said John Henry.

After that Cap'n Walters sent John Henry home to rest up for the match. When John Henry told Pollie Ann about it, she didn't like it a bit.

She said, "I wish that John Hardy would keep away. I don't like the idea of you messin' around with a steam drill."

All the same, she fixed him up a good snack, the way she always did. She even made some hot biscuits. John Henry ate hearty, then went to bed. He had him a good sleep and got up while it was still dark.

By the time John Henry and Pollie Ann reached the mountain the red morning sun was in the sky. Word about the race had got around, and a crowd had come from town to see the fun. Breezy Sam was standing by the steam drill, watching John Hardy get up steam.

The drivers and shakers cheered as they saw John Henry. None of them was going to work that day except Li'l Willie, and some blacksmiths to put points on the jumpers.

In a little while Cap'n Walters and Breezy Sam put their heads together. Then they called to John Henry and John Hardy both.

"Listen close," said Cap'n Walters. "When I give the signal, you start. At the end of twelve hours you'll stop. The

128

one that drives the deepest hole in the rock wins. Now get set, and good luck."

"I don't need luck, cap'n," said John Hardy. "I got the steam drill."

"I don't need a steam drill," laughed John Henry. "I got my hammer."

John Henry whipped off his shirt. He rubbed some rock dust on his hands, and a little on the handle of his hammer. He waited until Li'l Willie had knelt at his feet with the jumper.

"Let 'er go, cap'n!" he said.

"Ready, cap'n!" cried John Hardy from the seat of the steam drill.

"Go!" yelled Cap'n Walters, and the match was on.

"Drive that steel, John Henry!" shouted Pollie Ann.

"Do it, John Henry!" said the drivers and shakers. "Whop that steel, brother! Mash it down, man!"

Some of the folks from the town cheered the steam drill.

"Beat him down, John Hardy!" they said. "Beat that John Henry down!"

The steam drill went chug-chug and John Henry sang:

> Hear my hammer
> Ring like silver,
> Shake this jumper,
> Turn this jumper,
> I got a rainbow
> Round my shoulder,
> Soon we blow
> This mountain down.

Both John Henry and John Hardy worked sure and steady. By the time the sun was shining bright, they were about even. Li'l Willie reached for a five-foot jumper and John Hardy changed his drill.

"How you feel, high pockets?" said John Hardy.

"Feel fine, low pockets," answered John Henry. "Just workin' up a sweat."

Breezy Sam yelled, "You, John Hardy! Show him a bit

of real speed! Let that double-jointed steam drill loose, boy!"

John Hardy let out the steam drill full blast, and that steam drill really began to drill. For a couple of minutes she chugged away, then *bam!* she stopped. John Hardy had started it too fast and ruined a drill.

"Now's your chance, John Henry!" said Pollie Ann. "Get way ahead while he's changin' drills."

"That's just what I had in mind," answered John Henry. And he sang out to Li'l Willie:

> *Come on, Li'l Willie,*
> *Hold her steady,*
> *Turn her round,*
> *Shake her good.*
> *Let's beat that steam drill down,*
> *Lawd, Lawd, let's beat that steam drill down.*

Li'l Willie held the jumper steady. He turned her round and shook her good. And John Henry whopped it on down.

Breezy Sam's face was as red as a ripe tomato, while Cap'n Walters was just all smiles. But at last John Hardy got the steam drill started again, and he did it right. By the time the noonday sun was high in the sky, he was even with John Henry. Yes, he was even and inching ahead.

John Henry brought his hammer down so fast it threw sparks. Li'l Willie had to pour water on the jumper to keep it from getting too hot. Still, John Henry couldn't seem to gain on the steam drill. By the time the afternoon sun was blazing down, the steam drill was in the lead.

John Henry stood up straight and threw down his hammer.

"Great day!" roared John Hardy. "He's quittin' the race! I win!"

"You hush your big mouth!" said Pollie Ann. "John Henry ain't quittin' a-tall."

"That's right," said John Henry quietly, taking the head off his hammer. He pulled a long length of rawhide from his pocket and looped it through the hammerhead. Then he picked up a spare hammerhead, took out another length of

132

rawhide, and did the same.

"Now, Li'l Willie," he said, "hold that jumper good and steady, 'cause I'm goin' to hammer in double-quick time."

And he started swinging those hammerheads by the rawhide, one in his left hand and one in his right. The two hammerheads came down on the jumper, ringing like a pair of bells.

John Hardy made his steam drill run as fast as he could. It shook and shivered, biting through the rock. Under the burning hot sun the steam drill drilled and John Henry drove that steel. And by the time the sun was red in the west, John Henry had caught up with the steam drill.

Then he stopped swinging those two hammerheads. He put one head back on the handle and began using one hammer again.

"How do you feel, son?" asked Cap'n Walters.

"Is your strength runnin' out, John Henry?" asked Pollie Ann.

John Henry shook his head and went on hammering. There wasn't any sound but the chug of the steam drill and the clang of John Henry's hammer. Everybody else was still— Pollie Ann and Li'l Willie, Cap'n Walters and Breezy Sam, the drivers and the shakers and the folks from the town. Because it was the flesh against the steam, the flesh against the steam. And a man was nothing but a man, and there was no telling how long John Henry would last.

"How come it so quiet?" said John Henry. He sang out, sweet and mellow:

> O my shaker, why don't you sing?
> For I'm throwing forty pounds from my hips on down,
> Just you hear that cold steel ring,
> That cold steel ring.

Li'l Willie started to sing, then stopped. John Henry was breathing hard now. He gave a little moan every time he raised his hammer. But he didn't leave off whopping that steel.

Pollie Ann whispered to Cap'n Walters, "How much time is left, cap'n? Look at your watch, cap'n, 'cause my John Henry's strength is running out."

"Half a minute to go," said Cap'n Walters, his eyes on his watch. "Quarter of a minute . . . ten seconds . . . five . . ." He raised his hand and shouted, "Time's up! The match is over!"

John Hardy stopped the steam drill. John Henry stood up straight, and his shadow stretched out long over the mountain.

The next minute the crowd let out a mighty cheer. They could see John Henry had drilled deeper into the rock. They gathered around him, cheering and laughing and carrying on.

"I knew you'd beat the steam drill!" said Cap'n Walters.

"We all knew it!" said the drivers and shakers.

John Henry looked down on them and smiled. He raised his hand and slowly passed it over his eyes. Then he crumpled up and fell to the ground.

"I said I'd beat the steam drill," he said. "But a man ain't nothin' but a man."

"Send for a doctor, Cap'n Walters!" cried Pollie Ann.

Before the cap'n could answer, John Henry's head fell back.

"No use to call a doctor," said Cap'n Walters quietly. "John Henry's gone, died with his hammer in his hand."

A chill wind blew across the mountain as the evening sun went down. All the men took off their hats. While Pollie Ann let out a great sob, they picked up John Henry. Walking slow, they carried him down to his little house. There wasn't any box big enough to hold John Henry, so they laid him out in

134

a box car. They couldn't get the box car into John Henry's house, so they strung up a tent. And they left John Henry with Pollic Ann.

All night long Pollie Ann sat beside him. She lit a candle, and she had nobody to talk to but her shadow. She kept sobbing and saying, "It don't seem as if it could be. I can't believe John Henry ain't no more."

It was close to morning when she heard a little moan.

"Who's that?" she said.

After that she heard a little groan.

Pollie Ann turned her head, looking at the box car. And great day in the morning, if John Henry wasn't sitting up and raising his head! He was, and that's a fact!

"John Henry!" shrieked Pollie Ann. "You ain't dead!"

"Not so's I could notice it," said John Henry. "What caused you to think I was?"

Pollie Ann told him.

"I just threw me a faint," said John Henry.

"Mighty powerful faint," said Pollie Ann.

"I'm a mighty powerful man," said John Henry. "And when I faint, I don't faint puny."

He started to climb out of the box car, but Pollie Ann had to help him. John Henry wasn't dead, but he felt poorly. His strength was gone, and he was sort of sunken in and shriveled up.

Pollie Ann put him to bed and said, "Just rest yourself. You'll get back your strength in no time. I'll just call off the buryin'. I wonder could we turn it into a party, seein' that you're alive."

John Henry shook his head.

"No, ma'am!" he said. "Don't you do that, Pollie Ann!"

"Why not, John Henry?"

"Without my strength I ain't the man I was," said John Henry. "Why, if John Hardy was to see me this way, I'd never hear the end of it. I don't want to hear him laughin' 'cause the steam drill wore me down. You just let folks go on thinkin' I ain't on this earth no more. Then when I'm feelin' good again, I'll pick up my hammer and run John Hardy and his steam drill right into the ground."

Pollie Ann didn't like it. She didn't like making believe she was a widow woman and telling folks something that wasn't so. But she was so glad to have John Henry back she didn't want to cross him. While he ate the snack she fixed, she filled the box car with rocks.

"Put in plenty," John Henry said. "Weigh it down, so nobody will know I ain't inside."

Peeping through the window, he saw folks coming toward the tent. He told Pollie Ann to put on her black veil and stand beside the box car.

John Henry watched the folks streaming into the tent. Cap'n Walters was there, with Li'l Willie and the drivers, the shakers, and the blacksmiths. They all carried flowers to strew over him. John Hardy and Breezy Sam followed, with the most flowers of all. Then came folks from all over the town.

John Henry chuckled when he saw John Hardy's long face.

"I declare," he said. "That John Hardy is makin' out like he lost his best friend."

Pretty soon John Henry heard the folks singing *Swing Low Sweet Chariot* and *Deep River*. He sang right along with them. Then the preacher said a few words and John Henry listened.

"Sisters and brethern," said the preacher, "John Henry was a man. He was a big man and a natural man. Still, he wasn't nothin' but a man, and now he's gone. He's gone to where he won't ever have to drive steel no more."

"I ain't gone," John Henry said. "All the same, that's nice preachin'."

The tears came to John Henry's eyes as he listened to the preacher. He was still sniffling when the folks came out of the tent. Fifty of them wore white gloves and carried the box car on their shoulders. They put the box car on a wagon frame drawn by thirty-two black horses. They heaped it with flowers, then a band played slow music and the procession started on its way.

Soon as everybody was out of sight, John Henry crept from his bed. He went to the corner, where his hammer was leaning against the wall. He put both hands on the handle, but he couldn't lift it at all. No matter how hard he tried, he couldn't budge that hammer an inch.

John Henry shuffled over to the piano, feeling sad. He played a few chords and began to sing the weary blues:

I beat the steam drill, but see what it did to me,
Beat the ol' steam drill, but look what it did to me,
John Henry ain't the man he used to be.

He was still at it when Pollie Ann came back.

She took one look at him and burst out, "You, John Henry —you get back in your bed! No need to sing the blues. Just lay back easy while I fix you a snack. You'll fatten up and soon you'll be back on the mountain again."

"But what are we goin' to do? How we goin' to live?" asked John Henry.

"Well," said Pollie Ann, "I can't drive steel on the mountain. But I reckon I can drive steel where they're layin' track. I'll get me a job till you're on your feet again."

And that's just what she did. While John Henry lay on his bed, Pollie Ann drove steel like a man. As soon as she got home she'd fix John Henry a snack of hog jowls, chittlin's, cracklin's, corn pone, side meat, and greens. And John Henry began to fatten up. He began to get his strength back, too. Every day he tried to lift his hammer, and each day he could raise it a little more. And one day he found he could give it a full swing—not the way he used to, maybe, but better than anybody he knew.

"Just need a little practice," he thought.

Then he had an idea. He'd walk up the mountain and get his job back from Cap'n Walters. He'd surprise Pollie Ann and John Hardy and anybody else who happened to be around.

"It'll be just like old times," he chuckled.

So he put on his overalls and his clodhopper shoes. Shouldering his hammer, he set off for the mountain. He kept laughing all the way, figuring how everybody would be surprised.

But as John Henry climbed the mountain he heard a sound: chug-chug, chuga-chug. John Henry stopped. Although the sun was blazing down on his back, a little shiver ran through him. He climbed on slowly, rounded a bend, and stopped again.

"Oh, my," he moaned.

Because he didn't hear any hammers ringing on the steel. He didn't see any drivers or any shakers. All he heard was chuga-chug-chug. All he could see was steam drills working away. And handling the biggest, loudest steam drill was John Hardy.

"Cap'n Walters!" called John Henry softly.

Cap'n Walters wasn't around either. There was a new cap'n, and he said, "He's not here, son. What can I do for you?"

"Cap'n," said John Henry, "I'm John Henry and—"

The cap'n threw back his head and laughed.

"Boy," he said, "what are you telling me? You're big all right, but you're not John Henry. Everybody knows he died with his hammer in his hand. And if he hadn't died, he wouldn't be driving steel on this mountain. All we use now are steam drills. And even with the steam drills, we're having a hard time pushing through the Big Bend Tunnel."

"Thank you, cap'n. Good day, suh," said John Henry.

Without another word he started walking away. He stumbled across the ground like a man who's had too much rye whiskey. His shoulders sagged, and he sort of settled into himself, shriveled and shrunken up.

At the edge of a cliff he stood for a minute. He tossed away his hammer, watching it drop till it was out of sight.

"Good-by, ol' hammer," he said. "You won't never ring on the mountain no more."

John Henry kept on walking till he got to his house. He sat down at the piano and played and sang:

Oh, they're usin' steam on the mountain—can't deny it,
    'cause it's true,
Yes, usin' steam on the mountain—can't deny it, 'cause
    it's true,
Ain't nothin' left in the world for a natural man to do.

It was the meanest, weariest, saddest, low-down blues anybody had ever sung. When Pollie Ann came in John Henry asked her why she hadn't told him about the steam drills.

"I didn't know," she said. "Anyway, you can drive steel on the railroad."

"I couldn't do that," said John Henry. "Not after driving steel on the mountain."

"Well, then, you could roust cotton," said Pollie Ann.

"No," said John Henry. "Not after drivin' steel on the railroad."

"How about pickin' cotton?"

"Couldn't pick cotton," said John Henry. "Not after I rousted it on the Mississippi."

"John Henry," said Pollie Ann, "why don't you run one of these steam drills, then?"

John Henry shook his head.

"That's no work for a natural man," he said. "Don't take

a man to run a machine. Why, a machine's got no beat. You could never make up a song for it. No, there ain't nothin' left for a natural man, nothin' a-tall."

"What are you goin' to do?" asked Pollie Ann.

"Travel around," said John Henry. "Travel around, till I wear myself down and end out my days. 'Cause there's no place left in this world for a natural man no more."

So John Henry and Pollie Ann started traveling around. From West Virginia to East Virginia, to New Orleans, Kansas City, St. Louis, and Chicago. Kalamazoo, Louisville, Chattanooga, and Memphis—they went there too. They wandered and they rambled and they traveled around.

Nobody knew John Henry was John Henry. He got more shriveled up and shrunken in every day. He picked up a little

money working as a janitor, bellhop, or something like that. Pollie Ann worked too, as a cook or a maid. And whatever they did or wherever they went, John Henry never sang anything but the mean, weary, sad, low-down blues.

In Memphis John Henry and Pollie Ann both got jobs in a restaurant. John Henry waited on table, while Pollie Ann cooked snacks for the folks. Once in a while John Henry would walk over to the piano and sing a blues.

He'd just finished singing one day when he saw a man sitting in a corner. The air was blue with cigarette smoke, so John Henry couldn't make out his face. Anyway, he was hunched over the table with his head in his hands.

Walking over to him, John Henry said, "Anybody get your order? What would you like?"

"There's plenty I'd like," said the man. "But I can't eat a thing. I got the blues, just like you said in the song. Yes, sir—I got the John Henry blues, what I mean."

"What you got to do with John Henry?" asked John Henry.

"Ever hear of the Big Bend Tunnel?" asked the man, still holding his head in his hands.

"I heard tell of it," said John Henry.

"Well," said the man, "I've been runnin' a steam drill on the mountain, but I ain't runnin' it no more. The tunnel isn't even halfway finished, but the cap'n laid me off. Said he's goin' to get some real men to run those steam drills—men who can blow down a hard rock mountain. But I know he can't. Couldn't anybody push that mountain down but John Henry, and he's a long time gone."

Then he dropped his hands from his face, and great day in the morning, if it wasn't John Hardy! And that John Hardy looked hard at John Henry. He shook his head a little. He wrinkled his forehead. He rubbed his eyes and he looked again.

John Henry didn't waste any time. He ran to the kitchen, then through it, calling to Pollie Ann. Before they could reach the door, though, John Hardy caught up with them.

"John Henry!" yelled John Hardy. "I don't know how it came about! I know you ain't the same! But you're John Henry and you ain't dead! Yes, suh! And right beside you is Pollie Ann."

John Henry stopped and heaved a sigh.

"All right, John Hardy," he said. "I'm John Henry, and you've found me. Now go on and have your laugh."

John Hardy didn't even snicker. He just kept looking at John Henry and listened while Pollie Ann told what had happened.

"Just like a country boy," he said.

"Lookie here, small fry!" said John Henry.

"Huh!" said John Hardy. "You ain't such a big fry your-self no more. Now you listen to me. You've got to go back to West Virginia. You run one of those steam drills and push that mountain down."

"John Hardy," said Pollie Ann, "I always thought you was a no-'count big mouth. But now you talkin' sense."

But John Henry shook his head.

He said, "No, I ain't the natural man I was. And I couldn't run a steam drill. Why, a steam drill is a machine, and it ain't got no beat. I couldn't make up a song for it, let alone work it."

"You crazy, boy," said John Hardy. "A machine *has* got a beat. Only you never listened to it."

And then Pollie Ann really told John Henry off.

"John Henry!" she burst out. "You were too proud to let folks know you'd lost your strength, so I had to make believe I was a widow woman. Then you found out about them usin' steam drills, and you felt sorry for yourself. Now you're still a man, and there's always a place for a natural man. You beat the steam drill, but you ain't really licked it. That's what you got to do. Now get along."

"Maybe," said John Henry.

"No maybe about it," said Pollie Ann. "You get goin', and no foolin'."

John Henry looked at Pollie Ann, and he looked at John Hardy. He looked back at Pollie Ann again, and he said, "Yes, ma'am."

The very next minute he was on his way out of the café. Together with Pollie Ann and John Hardy, he traveled back to West Virginia. Every time they passed a factory with machines, John Hardy would get John Henry to listen. John

Henry put one hand behind his ear and heard the wheels go clackety-clack. He heard the motors go hum-hum-hum. He heard the pistons go pumpety-pump.

"I do declare," he said. "They sure enough got a beat."

And John Henry began to walk straighter and taller. By the time they reached West Virginia he was halfway back to his natural size.

In the dead of night John Henry and John Hardy climbed up the mountain. John Henry studied the steam drill, learning how it worked. John Hardy showed him how to fire the boiler, and they practiced drilling the rock. John Henry listened close as the steam puffed, the wheels turned, and the engine went chugety-chug-chug.

"I can't deny it," he said. "It's got a beat. It ain't like my ol' hammer ringin' on the steel, but I'm gettin' to like it."

Every day John Henry and John Hardy lay low, not letting anybody see them. Nights they practiced with the steam drill. And at last they were really ready to push through the tunnel. They just walked up the mountain one morning and John Henry started drilling away.

When the cap'n showed up he bellowed, "What do you think you're doin'? Get away from that steam drill! I never hired you! Come on, boy, before I get the law on you!"

"Go get the law, cap'n," said John Henry. "But before you do I'm goin' to blow this mountain down. 'Cause I'm John Henry, the natural man, and I'm goin' to push through this Big Bend Tunnel."

And he sang:

> There ain't no steam drill
> On this mountain,
> Can chug like mine, boys,
> Chug like mine.

This ol' steam drill
Chug like thunder,
Drill like lightnin',
Yes, indeed!

While the cap'n and all his gang watched with their mouths open, John Henry let out the steam full blast. He ran the steam drill just right, drilling faster, harder, and deeper than anybody before or since.

"Stand back, folks!" said John Henry. "Stand back, 'cause I'm a big man and gettin' bigger every minute! I'm a natural man, and I'm gettin' naturaler every second! Stand back, 'cause I'm goin' to blast this tunnel out in no time!"

Soon as John Henry drilled a hole, he and John Hardy filled it with dynamite. They blasted out the rocks and cleared them away in no time.

The cap'n sat back on his heels and scratched his head.

"Don't know if he's John Henry or not," he said. "Don't know if I should allow this or not. But no matter who, what, or why, this man can sure handle a steam drill."

All day long John Henry worked, stopping once to eat a snack Pollie Ann brought him. He blasted, he cleared away, and he drilled. He drilled and blasted and cleared away. Come night and he and John Hardy kept right on.

The stars shone out in the sky, but you couldn't tell them from the sparks that flew from the steam drill. The chug of the drill and the thunder of the blasting was heard for miles around. Folks listened, then hurried up the mountain to see what it was all about.

"Looks like John Henry," they said. "Couldn't be, though. Unless it's his ghost."

"Couldn't any ghost drill like that," said the cap'n. "And if that's not John Henry, that's John Henry's twin."

"That's John Henry, all right," said Pollie Ann. "And ain't he a natural man?"

At last the sky began to pale and the morning star to fade. John Henry drilled the last hole. He blasted the last blast. There was a great noise, and when the dust had cleared

everybody saw the tunnel had been pushed through. And
the folks sang:

> *John Henry's back on the mountain,*
> *Though you can't hear his hammer ring,*
> *He's chugging away on a steam drill now,*
> *He's driving steel again.*

> *And every time that steam drill drills*
> *You can hear his cap'n shout,*
> *And every time that steam drill drills*
> *A thousand stars fly out.*

> *John Henry's built a tunnel*
> *For the locomotives and the cars,*
> *John Henry's back on the mountain,*
> *He's whoppin' out the stars.*

John Henry asked John Hardy, "How'd I do, small fry?"
"Just fine, tall fry," answered John Hardy.

"Couldn't be finer," said Pollie Ann, and the cap'n said
the same.

All of a sudden they heard a noise. The steam drill was
puffing and panting, moaning and groaning. It shook and
shivered as if all its bolts were loose.

John Henry took a deep breath. He stood up tall, almost
as tall as a box car is long. He stretched his arms, and they
were thicker than the cross-ties on the railroad. In the light
of the rising sun his black skin shone like a new pair of ten-
dollar shoes.

John Henry looked hard at the steam drill, singing:

> *I've laid aside my hammer,*
> *I say it just as plain,*
> *But I've run the steam drill into the ground*
> *And I'm a natural man again.*

Just as John Henry sang the last note, there was a loud crash. Every nut, bolt and screw flew off the steam drill. While the folks laughed and cheered, it buckled up and fell down—because John Henry had run the steam drill right into the ground.

STEAMBOAT BILL

AND THE CAPTAIN'S
TOP HAT *BY*

IRWIN SHAPIRO

PICTURES BY DONALD McKAY

Y ou may think that the boilers of the Whippoorwill exploded and blew Steamboat Bill to bits. But they didn't. You may think that Steamboat Bill never did beat the record of the Robert E. Lee. But he did. Of course, he almost didn't, because of a little trouble he had with Captain Carter.

The whole thing started when the Whippoorwill came steaming into St. Louis one bright sunny day. And a grand sight the Whippoorwill was, with her white decks shining in the sun and her smokestacks spouting black smoke. Steamboat Bill was at the wheel in the pilot house, which is where a pilot should be. He had a big cigar in his mouth. His coat was open to show his fancy checked vest. His cap was perched on the back of his head, and his gray hair flew in the breeze. Anybody could see that he was a mighty man.

After the Whippoorwill rounded the bend, Steamboat rang the big brass landing-bell. With his other hand he pulled a lever, letting loose a blast of the five-toned whistle. Then he

put both hands on the wheel and eased the *Whippoorwill* up to the levee, as gentle as a mother with a baby.

"Prettiest landing I ever did see," said the second pilot. He was a young fellow with a big droopy mustache. His name was Sam Clemens.

"Thank you, Sam," said Steamboat. "Thank you kindly. But I guess the captain will be along soon with a different story."

And sure enough, there was Captain Carter striding toward them on the hurricane deck. He was wearing a tail coat and a top hat.

Now Captain Carter and Steamboat Bill were great friends. But at the end of every trip, they had a quarrel. If Captain Carter didn't start it, Steamboat did. They said it was the only way they could keep each other from getting swelled heads. To tell the truth, they enjoyed quarreling with each

other. And since they always
made up afterward, no harm
was done.

Captain Carter threw open
the door of the pilot house.

"Pilot," he said, "now that the voyage is over, I've something to say to you."

"Say it quick and say it quiet," said Steamboat.

"I'll say it any way I like," said Captain Carter. "And this
is what I have to say. Didn't you take that last bend a little
too fast?"

"The law of these United States says that a captain cannot
give orders to a pilot," answered Steamboat slowly.

"Only when the pilot is on duty," the captain came back,
quick as a shot. "Anyway, laws be blowed! Did you or didn't
you take that last bend too fast?"

"I'll answer to no captain, you thundering dunderhead!"
shouted Steamboat.

"I'm a dunderhead, am I?" said Captain Carter. "Then
you're a bomickle!"

"I'm a bomickle, am I?" said Steamboat. "Then you're a
comickle!"

"So I'm a comickle, eh?" said the captain.

Steamboat shoved his face close to the captain's.

"Aye," he said. "You're a comickle."

"Enough of your sass!" burst out Captain Carter. And taking off his top hat, he threw it on the floor. "Kick that," he said, the way you would dare somebody to knock a chip off your shoulder. "Kick it and get what's coming to you. Go on, you ring-tailed baboon, give it just one little kick."

"I've a good mind to do that very thing," said Steamboat.

"That's just what I'm asking you to do."

"But I won't take orders from a captain!" roared Steamboat. "I wouldn't kick your hat if you left it there a million years!"

"In that case," said the captain, "I'll forget everything you said."

"And if that's the way you feel about it," said Steamboat, "I'll forget everything you said."

Captain Carter began to smile. Steamboat Bill began to smile. They shook hands, and pretty soon they were laughing and slapping each other on the back.

Sam Clemens came over to them with a handful of cigars.

"Have a cigar, gentlemen?" he asked.

"Thank you, Sam," said Steamboat, taking a cigar.

"Don't mind if I do," said Captain Carter.

The three of them stood there, laughing and smoking their cigars.

At last Steamboat said, "Well, gentlemen, I guess I'll look around a bit. I'll see you later at the Slocum House."

"Fine," said Captain Carter.

"Fine," said Sam.

Steamboat Bill left the boat and started walking along the levee. Boats were drawn up along the wharves. There was the *Natchez* and the *Tuscarora*, the *A. L. Shotwell* and the *Duke*

of Orleans. The *Natchez* was loading cargo. The rousters sang
a song as they carried sacks of meal up the gangplank.

"Up sack, you gone! Up sack, you gone!" sang the rousters.

The chief mate shouted, "Hump yourselves, boys! Get
those sacks on board!"

From all sides people called out to Steamboat.

"Hello, Steamboat!" they said. "How are you, Steamboat
Bill? Good day, sir!"

"How's the river at Hat Island?" asked the pilot of the
Duke of Orleans.

"How's the crossing at Memphis?" asked the pilot of the
Tuscarora.

"How's the river at Twelve-Mile Point?" asked the pilot of
the *A. L. Shotwell.*

"She's slack water all along," answered Steamboat Bill.
"Couldn't get through the cut-out at Hat Island. The reef is
showing at Twelve-Mile Point."

The pilots nodded.

"Steamboat knows the river like he knows the palm of his own hand," they said.

Steamboat smiled. He opened his coat to show his fancy checked vest. He pushed out his chest, pulled his cap over one eye, and puffed his cigar. Anyone could see that he was a mighty man.

Steamboat was still talking to the pilots when Captain Carter came running up. The captain's face was as long as a gangplank.

"What's the matter, Captain?" asked Steamboat.

"Have you heard the news?" said the captain. "There's trouble at Fort Sumter."

"That's bad," said Steamboat, frowning.

"That's bad," said all the pilots, and they shook their heads.

"Steamboat," said Captain Carter, "it means war. Civil war."

"Aye," said Steamboat. "Civil war."

For a long time no one spoke. Then Steamboat said, "Captain, are you with the North or the South?"

"I'm with the South," answered Captain Carter. "A state has the right to leave the Union."

"I'm with the North," said Steamboat. "The states must be united."

Steamboat and Captain Carter looked at each other.

"Good-by, Steamboat," said Captain Carter, holding out his hand. "And good luck."

Steamboat shook the captain's hand.

"Good-by, Captain," he said. "And good luck to you."

Then Captain Carter walked back to the *Whippoorwill*, and Steamboat Bill walked away from the levee.

IT WAS a long time before Steamboat saw the captain again. But everything must come to an end, even wars. And so one bright sunny day, Steamboat hurried down to the levee at St. Louis to meet the captain.

As Steamboat hurried along, people called out to him from every side.

"Hello, Steamboat!" they said. "How are you, Steamboat Bill! Good day, sir!"

Steamboat smiled such a big smile that it almost hid his face.

"Hello, friends," he said. "I'm feeling very well. The civil war is over and Captain Carter is coming back on the *Whippoorwill*."

Steamboat opened his coat to show his fancy checked vest. He pushed out his chest and pulled his cap over one eye. Anyone could see that he was a mighty man.

Suddenly someone cried out, "Here she comes! Here comes the *Whippoorwill*."

Everyone ran down to the wharf to see the *Whippoorwill* come in. Carts and wagons clattered. Dogs barked. Boys whistled and yelled. When Steamboat saw the *Whippoorwill* steaming around the bend, he was so excited he could hardly stand still. Yes, there she was! Her white decks were as clean as a Dutch kitchen. Her brass-work shone in the sun like a new penny. Her five-toned whistle was blowing, and black smoke poured out of her smokestacks.

Kerplunk! Her gangplank hit the land, and a man in a white apron came running down. He was carrying a tray loaded with nuts, ices, grapes, pineapples and oranges.

"Compliments of the captain," he said.

The crowd rushed over to him. Soon there wasn't a thing left on the tray. Everyone stood around, munching and laughing.

"Where's Captain Carter?" asked Steamboat.

"He'll be here directly," said the man.

And sure enough, there was Captain Carter coming down the gangplank. He was wearing his tail coat and top hat. He walked straight up to Steamboat Bill.

"Well, Steamboat?" said Captain Carter.

"Well, Captain?" said Steamboat.

The next minute they were laughing and slapping each other on the back.

"It's good to see you again, Steamboat," said Captain Carter.

"You're a sight for sore eyes, Captain," said Steamboat. "And so is the *Whippoorwill*."

"She's a fine boat," said the captain proudly. "And soon you'll be at her wheel again. That is, if you still want to be my pilot."

"I wouldn't pilot for anyone else," said Steamboat, "and you know it."

Captain Carter gave Steamboat a tremendous thump on the back.

"And I wouldn't have anyone else for a pilot," he said. "Yes, sir, we'll both be back on the *Whippoorwill* again. It will be just like old times. You were for the North and I was for the South, but the war is over and we'll forget all about it."

"We won't even talk about it," said Steamboat.

"Not a word," agreed the captain. "The North won, and that's all there is to it. But I must say we gave you boys a battle at Bull Run."

"That's right. But we certainly had you on the run at Shiloh," chuckled Steamboat.

The captain laughed.

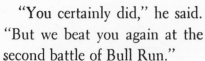

"You certainly did," he said. "But we beat you again at the second battle of Bull Run."

"We won at Vicksburg."

"Yes, but we whaled the tar out of you at Fredericksburg. And we fooled you at Chancellorsville."

"We won again at Gettysburg," said Steamboat.

"That's because you were lucky," said the captain.

"Lucky?" said Steamboat. "How about Missionary Ridge? I suppose we were lucky to win that one, too."

"Well, you would have lost if it hadn't been so foggy."

Steamboat was beginning to get angry.

"Next you'll be telling me that Grant didn't take Richmond," he said.

"Just luck, that's all," said the captain.

"Is that a fact?" said Steamboat.

"Yes, that's a fact!" shouted Captain Carter.

"And I suppose the South won the war!" Steamboat shouted back at him.

"We should have won!"

Steamboat looked the captain up and down.

"Captain Carter," he said, "you're a poor loser, that's what you are!"

"Shouldn't have lost!" shouted the captain.

"JOHNNY REB!" roared Steamboat.

"YANKEE!" roared the captain.

One of the men in the crowd said, "Gentlemen! This is no way to act."

"It's not my fault," said Steamboat. "This baboon wants to fight the war all over again."

"I'm not a baboon!" shouted the captain. "And I've stood enough!" And taking off his hat, he threw it on the ground. "Kick that," he said to Steamboat. "Go ahead. Just one little kick!"

"I've a good mind to do that very thing," said Steamboat.

"That's what I'm asking you to do."

"Then by the Great Horn Spoon, I will!" roared Steamboat. And he gave the captain's top hat a great kick. It sailed high into the air and fell into the river with a PLOP.

Captain Carter watched his top hat float down the river until it was out of sight.

"Steamboat," he said, "this is the end. You'll never pilot the *Whippoorwill* again. You're no friend of mine."

And with that Captain Carter walked up the gangplank.

"Steamboat, aren't you going to make up with the Captain?" asked someone in the crowd.

Steamboat pulled his cap down over one eye and lit a cigar.

"Captain Carter started this quarrel," he said, "and he'll have to end it. If he wants to talk to me, he knows where I'll be."

And he started walking toward the Slocum House.

WHEN Steamboat Bill left his room the next morning, he found a crowd of captains and owners waiting to see him. There was the owner of the *Eclipse* and the captain of the *Dexter;* the captain of the *Sultana* and the owner of the *Magnolia;* the captain of the *Southern Belle* and the owner of the *Belle of the West.* They all wanted Steamboat for a pilot.

They followed Steamboat down the hall. They walked with him down the stairs. They sat beside him as he ate his breakfast. Steamboat just shook his head.

"I guess Captain Carter will be along soon and ask me to come back on the *Whippoorwill,*" he said.

But Captain Carter didn't. He just kept the same pilot and took the *Whippoorwill* down to New Orleans.

"Oh, well," said Steamboat. "He'll come to see me on his next trip. He's a proud man and he has a temper, but he'll cool off."

The next time the *Whippoorwill* came to St. Louis, Steamboat hurried down to the levee. He stood where Captain

Carter would be sure to see him. But when the captain came down the gangplank, he walked past Steamboat as though he weren't there at all.

The same thing happened on the *Whippoorwill's* next trip, and on the trip after that.

"You'd better get yourself another job," the captains and owners told Steamboat. "Captain Carter's temper is worse than ever. He throws down his top hat ten times a day. His temper is so bad that no pilot wants to work for him. The only pilots he can get are Caleb Smith and Jim Johnson."

"Why, Caleb Smith is so old he can hardly get around," said Steamboat.

"That's right," said the owners and captains.

"And Jim Johnson is just a youngster," said Steamboat.

"That's right," said the owners and captains.

"In that case," said Steamboat, "I guess Captain Carter will soon ask me to come back on the *Whippoorwill.*"

But Steamboat was wrong. Captain Carter didn't even say hello to Steamboat when he saw him on the levee.

Steamboat felt so bad that he never went down to the levee again. He stayed in his room all day. He would look out the window at the clouds of black smoke floating across the city. When he got tired looking out the window he listened to the bells and whistles of the boats on the river. When he was tired of listening, he read the newspaper. And when he was tired of reading the newspaper, he looked out the window again.

Then came the day when the *Natchez* and the *Robert E. Lee* finished their race from New Orleans. Steamboat was looking out the window, as usual. He could hear the crowds cheer as the *Robert E. Lee* came steaming up the river.

A man ran down the street and shouted to Steamboat, "She broke the record! She made it from New Orleans in

174

three days, eighteen hours, and fourteen minutes!"

Steamboat slammed down the window.

"It should have been the *Whippoorwill* that broke the record," he said. Then he sighed, "But there's nothing I can do about it."

He tried not to hear the cheers of the crowd at the levee. He sat down and put his head in his hands. He was sitting that way when there was a knock at the door.

"Go away!" said Steamboat. "I don't want to see anybody!"

"This isn't anybody," said a voice. "This is Sam Clemens."

"Sam Clemens!" said Steamboat, and threw open the door. "Come in, Sam. How are you?"

"Fine," said Sam Clemens. "How are you, Steamboat? Here, have a cigar."

"Thank you kindly," said Steamboat. He puffed his cigar, smiled at Sam, and said, "What have you been doing since

you stopped being a pilot?"

"Oh, I've been working on a paper and writing stories."

"Hm," said Steamboat. "It seems to agree with you. You look fine. And your mustache is bigger than ever."

"Funny thing about the mustache," said Sam. "I don't like it. Never did like it. I cut it off every night before I go to bed. But as soon as my eyes are closed it sneaks back on me. When I get up in the morning, there it is, sitting under my nose and laughing in my face."

"Sam," said Steamboat, "that's a funny story, but I can't laugh at it. I don't feel much like laughing. I guess you know why."

"I guess I do, Steamboat," said Sam. "But I have some news for you. Captain Carter is going to race the *Whippoorwill* against the *Thunderbolt*. He says he's going to beat the record of the *Robert E. Lee*."

"What!" shouted Steamboat. He was so angry that he

threw his cap on the floor and kicked it across the room. "The *Whippoorwill* will never win that race. She's a mighty boat, but she has to be handled just right. And Captain Carter has such a temper that he can't get a good pilot. But I guess there's nothing I can do about it." And he sighed.

Sam pulled his mustache and puffed out a cloud of smoke.

"Steamboat," he said, "stop that sighing. You're going to New Orleans and you're going to get on board the *Whippoorwill*. I don't know how you'll do it, but you will. You're going to teach Captain Carter a lesson, and you're going to break the record of the *Robert E. Lee*. And if you don't, you're no friend of mine."

Sam jammed on his hat and left the room. Steamboat stared after him. He shook his head. Then he scratched it. Then he shook it again. After that he started to smile

"By the Great Horn Spoon, I'll do it," he said. "I'm a mighty man and I'll do it. I'm Steamboat Bill, and I'm going to beat the record of the *Robert E. Lee*."

Two weeks later Steamboat was walking down the levee at New Orleans. It was night, and a big yellow moon shone in the sky. The river was full of little golden dots and ripples. Steamboat listened to the water slapping against the shore, and took a deep breath of the river air.

"Nothing smells as good as a river," he said. "And there's no river that smells as good as the Mississippi."

He walked along the levee until he came to the *Whippoorwill*. Her white decks glistened in the moonlight, and her smokestacks stood up black against the pale sky.

"Aye, she's a mighty boat," said Steamboat, "and she's going to beat the record of the *Robert E. Lee*."

The *Thunderbolt* was at the wharf next to the *Whippoorwill*. Steamboat looked her over.

"She's a nice boat, too," he said, "but she'll never beat the record of the *Robert E. Lee.*" Then Steamboat bent down and picked up a stone. He drew back his arm and threw the stone at the far end of the *Whippoorwill.* It fell on the deck with a bump.

"Who's there?" shouted the watchman on the *Whippoorwill.* And picking up his lantern, he ran across the deck to see what had made the noise.

"I knew that would get him," chuckled Steamboat. He walked up the gangplank and slipped into the cabin. He opened the door of a stateroom and went in. Then he lay down on the bunk for a little nap.

When Steamboat woke up it was afternoon. Outside the rousters were loading the last of the cargo. As they carried bales of cotton up the gangplank, they sang, "Lift dat cotton, hop! Lift dat cotton, hop!"

"Hump yourselves, boys!" sang out the chief mate. "Get that cotton on board. We've a race to run today!"

Steamboat went to the window and looked out. There were people everywhere—standing on the levee, sitting on rooftops, leaning from windows. Clouds of black smoke floated out from the *Whippoorwill's* smokestacks.

The chief mate shouted, while the rousters sang, "De las' sack! De las' sack!" Bells clanged and whistles blew.

Steamboat drew back his head as Captain Carter came hurrying by. With him were old Caleb Smith and young Jim Johnson. Caleb hobbled along on a cane. Jim's face was pale. The captain himself looked worried and anxious.

"Won't they be surprised!" chuckled Steamboat, and stuck his head out again.

Just then two cannons boomed. A great shout went up from the crowd as the *Whippoorwill's* crew gathered on the forecastle. One of the crew, dressed in a red shirt, waved a little flag. The crew began to sing:

"Ring, bells, ring!
Blow, whistle, blow!
Up the muddy Mississippi,
Up the river we go."

On the *Thunderbolt* the crew were singing:

"Roll, river, roll!
Roll, river, roll!
Steamboat comin' round the bend,
Steamin' toward the journey's end,
Roll, river, roll!"

With a blast of whistles, the *Whippoorwill* and the *Thunderbolt* began to move up the river. Their engines puffed and chugged. Their paddle wheels churned the water. Steam hissed.

"Hooray!" shouted the crowd, and threw their hats in the air. "Hooray for the *Whippoorwill!* Hooray for the *Thunderbolt!* Hooray!"

The *Thunderbolt* made a big curve and headed up the river. The *Whippoorwill* started to make a curve too, but suddenly it went scooting across to the opposite bank. By the

time the pilot got her headed straight again, the *Thunderbolt* was out of sight. The crowd on the levee roared with laughter.

"Careful, old Caleb!" they shouted. "Careful, young Jim! Watch your top hat, Captain Carter!"

Steamboat had to laugh, too.

"I guess the pilot is a little excited," he said. "And Captain Carter must be as angry as a wet hen. But never fear. Steamboat Bill will soon be at the wheel, and we'll beat the record of the *Robert E. Lee!*"

All day long Steamboat sat in the stateroom, smoking one cigar after another. The *Whippoorwill* chugged and churned and chuffed up the river, but the pilot just couldn't get speed out of her. It began to look as though she never would catch up with the *Thunderbolt*. When night came the *Whippoorwill* picked up a raft loaded with wood for the furnace.

"It's time for me to give Captain Carter a little surprise," said Steamboat. He stood up and opened his coat to show his fancy checked vest. He pushed out his chest and pulled his cap over one eye. Then he left the stateroom and made his way to the pilot house.

Steamboat saw young Jim Johnson walking along the hurricane deck. He reached out his hand and touched Jim on the shoulder.

"Good evening, Jim," said Steamboat.

Jim whirled around.

"Steamboat Bill!" he said, his eyes popping out of his head. And without waiting for another word, he jumped overboard and started swimming for shore.

"I must have given the lad a fright," said Steamboat, and went into the pilot house. Old Caleb Smith was at the wheel.

"Good evening, Caleb," said Steamboat.

Caleb cupped a hand over his ear.

"Eh?" he said. "What say? You'll have to speak louder. Who is it?"

"It's Steamboat Bill," said Steamboat Bill in a loud, clear voice.

Caleb put on his spectacles and stared into Steamboat's face.

"Why, so it is," he said. "I'm mighty glad to see you,

Steamboat. Maybe you can help me. I'm too old to handle the *Whippoorwill* and Jim Johnson is too young. We should never have come on this trip. You're the only man can handle the *Whippoorwill* the way she ought to be handled."

"Thank you kindly," said Steamboat. "And now, Caleb, if you want me to take the wheel and win the race, I'll tell you what to do. Get on the raft and get to shore. Don't let Captain Carter see you."

"I'll do that thing," nodded Caleb. He shook Steamboat's hand, wished him luck, and hobbled away.

"Now then," said Steamboat, taking the wheel. He peered out at the river and rang for full speed ahead. He steered the *Whippoorwill* a little closer to shore.

"We're near Rat-tail Island," he said, "and the current close to shore is better for us. Especially the way the river is rising."

The *Whippoorwill* began to pick up speed.

"Ah," said Steamboat, "that's better."

Soon the texas-tender came in with some hot coffee.

"Steamboat Bill!" he shouted. "You're back! Hooray!" He ran out to tell the crew that Steamboat was at the wheel of the Whippoorwill again.

Steamboat sipped the hot coffee and smiled.

"I guess Captain Carter will be along soon," he said.

And sure enough, there was Captain Carter hurrying toward him on the hurricane deck. He was wearing his tail coat and top hat. He burst into the pilot house, and glared at Steamboat. "Good evening, Captain," said Steamboat. "Fine evening. Just right for a race."

"What's the meaning of this!" shouted Captain Carter.

"Before you say anything else, I want to remind you of

one thing," said Steamboat politely. "The law of these United States forbids a captain from giving orders to a pilot."

"You're no pilot of mine!" roared the captain. "Get off this boat! Where's Caleb Smith? Where's Jim Johnson?"

"They're both on shore, Captain," said Steamboat. "And I'm your pilot now, whether you like it or not."

Captain Carter looked as though he were going to burst. But he knew it was against the law for a captain to give orders to the pilot. He rushed out on the hurricane deck and jumped up and down with rage.

"A fine crew I've got!" he shouted. "A fine mate I've got!

Fine deck hands! Fine watchmen! Call yourselves river men? You're a bunch of baboons, that's what you are! Letting Steamboat sneak on board! Letting Caleb Smith and Jim Johnson sneak off board! You're a pack of ring-tailed baboons!" He took off his top hat and threw it on the deck. "Kick that!" he bellowed. "Come on, any of you! Give it just one little kick. I'll knock the stuffing out of the whole crew!"

"Easy, Captain," said one of the deck hands. "We'll win this race now that Steamboat Bill is at the wheel! He's a mighty man, and he knows the river like he knows the palm of his own hand."

Captain Carter picked up his hat.

"All right," he said. "Don't mind me. Run the boat to suit yourselves. Just go ahead and do what you want. But if Steamboat Bill gets you into trouble, don't come running to me."

He sat down on a coil of rope and folded his arms.

"Just go ahead," he said. "Do as you please. You'll be sorry."

ALL that night and all the next day Steamboat steered the *Whippoorwill* up the Mississippi. She was making real speed, but still she couldn't catch up with the *Thunderbolt*. When they got to Hat Island, Steamboat ordered the leadsman to make soundings.

"Mark Twain!" sang out the leadsman. "M-a-r-k twain! Quarter twain! Mark three! M-a-r-k thre-e-e-e!"

"Just as I thought," said Steamboat. "The river is rising. The floods are coming down the Mississippi. I'm going to try the cut-out at Hat Island. If we can make it, it will save us miles."

Steamboat headed the boat toward the cut-out. The water was rushing between the shore and Hat Island with a terrible roar. In the pale light of the sunset the water looked dark and fearful. It boiled and bubbled, it rushed and roared.

Steamboat called for more steam.

"You see!" cried Captain Carter. "He's going to go up the cut-out. We'll never make it! We'll all be drowned! What did I tell you!"

Nobody listened to the captain. The crew kept throwing wood on the fire in the furnace, trying to get up more steam.

Steamboat pushed his cap on the back of his head. He gripped the wheel firmly and took a long puff on his cigar. Anybody could see that he was a mighty man.

"Stand firm, lads!" he shouted. "Here we go!"

The *Whippoorwill* shook from stem to stern as she plunged into the cut-out. The engines moaned and groaned and hissed steam. The paddle wheels thrashed the water. But before she could get through the cut-out, the current caught her. The *Whippoorwill* began to spin around and around like a top.

"I knew it!" howled Captain Carter. "What did I tell you? It's the end! Steamboat Bill will kill us all!"

But Steamboat steered the boat around carefully and they

slid back out of the cut-out.

"Boys," said Steamboat to the crew, "we can make it but I'll need more steam."

The engineer shook his head. "We've used up all our wood, Steamboat," he said.

"Then chop up the furniture!" said Steamboat. "Chop up the chairs! Chop up the tables! Chop up all the woodwork! But give me more steam, for I'm Steamboat Bill and I'm out to beat the record of the *Robert E. Lee!*"

"You'll ruin my boat!" shouted Captain Carter. But the crew cheered. With axes and hatchets they chopped up the gilt chairs from the dining room. They broke up the mahogany tables. They ripped out the doors. They smashed bedsteads. They even tore up part of the floor. They chopped everything into kindling wood and built the biggest fire that ever was in the furnace of a steamboat. Higher and higher

went the flames, while the furnace glowed ruby-red. And the steam began to rise in the boilers.

"The boiler will explode!" said Captain Carter. "We'll all be blown to bits! We'll be drowned! I told you so! I told you so!"

One of the deck hands said, "Maybe we'll all be blown to bits. Maybe we'll all drown. But Steamboat Bill is the mightiest man on the Mississippi, and I'd just as soon drown with him as with anybody else."

"Thank you kindly," said Steamboat. He lit another cigar, gripped the wheel, and called for full steam ahead.

The crew threw more wood on the fire. Billows of smoke rolled out of the smokestacks. Sparks flew out like flying stars. The blaze of the furnace threw a red and yellow shine on the river. And the steam rose in the boilers.

Steamboat headed the *Whippoorwill* up the cut-out again. She went up a little way, then stopped.

Captain Carter jumped up and down with glee.

"I told you so!" he said. "I knew it! I warned you! The

boilers are going to explode! We'll all be drowned! Maybe
next time you'll listen to your captain instead of a good-for-
nothing pilot!"

Steamboat edged the boat a little to one side. He turned
the wheel just the tiniest bit, and the Whippoorwill pulled
clear of the current. Chugging and hissing, the Whippoorwill
shot forward and sped up the cut-out. Her paddle wheels cut
into the water. She went so fast that she almost flew in the
air. If she would have gone any faster, the crew would have
had to throw out an anchor to keep her in the water.

"Hooray!" shouted the crew. "We made it!"

"The race isn't over yet," grumbled Captain Carter. But he

thought to himself, "Maybe we *will* beat the record of the *Robert E. Lee*. Steamboat Bill is a stubborn baboon, but he's the mightiest pilot on the river."

The *Whippoorwill* went by the *Thunderbolt* like a hurricane. The *Thunderbolt's* crew heard a roar, felt a wind on their faces, and that was all.

"What was that?" asked the captain of the *Thunderbolt*.

"What was what?" asked his chief mate.

"I don't know," said the captain. "But it was something."

The *Whippoorwill* went steaming and roaring around the bend at St. Louis. Before anyone could say, "Here she comes," she was at the levee. Steamboat had to reverse the engines to get her to stop. Then he pulled the lever of the five-toned whistle. As the steam came rushing through the whistle, it let out a terrific blast. It was heard down the river as far as New Orleans, and up the river as far as Bemidji, Minnesota.

The crowd on the levee cheered and whistled and shouted and yelled. Steamboat Bill came out of the pilot house. He opened his coat to show his fancy checked vest. He pulled

193

his cap down over one eye and pushed out his chest. Anyone could see that he was a mighty man.

When the crowd saw him they cheered louder than ever.

"Hooray!" they said. "Hooray for Steamboat Bill! Hooray for the *Whippoorwill!* Hooray for Captain Carter! They beat the record of the *Robert E. Lee!*"

Captain Carter walked up to Steamboat. He walked slowly and he looked ashamed.

"Well, Captain?" said Steamboat.

"Well, Steamboat?" said the captain.

Steamboat Bill began to smile. Captain Carter began to smile.

The next minute they were shaking hands and slapping each other on the back.

"Steamboat," said the captain, "you're the mightiest man on the Mississippi. And I'm a stubborn old dunderhead. And a bomickle and a comickle as well. Also a ring-tailed baboon."

Captain Carter took off his top hat and threw it on the deck.

"Kick that," he said to Steamboat. "Go ahead. Kick it into the river."

Steamboat shook his head.

"Then I'll do it myself," said Captain Carter. And he gave

the top hat such a kick that it went sailing out into the river.

Steamboat Bill and Captain Carter walked down the gang-plank together. The crowd cheered and cheered as though it would never stop. All the steamboats at the levee blew their whistles. A brass band played "Hail to the Chief."

Then a man with a big droopy mustache pushed his way through the crowd. It was Sam Clemens.

He slapped Steamboat Bill on the back. He slapped Captain Carter on the back. He shook hands with them both.

"I knew you would beat the record of the *Robert E. Lee*," he said.

"Sam, I would never have done it if it hadn't been for you," said Steamboat. "It was your idea that put me on the *Whippoorwill*, and I'll never forget it."

Sam Clemens smiled. He reached in his pocket and took out a handful of cigars.

"Have a cigar, gentlemen," he said.

"Thank you kindly, Sam," said Steamboat, taking a cigar.

"Don't mind if I do," said Captain Carter.

Then, arm in arm, Steamboat and Sam and Captain Carter walked away from the levee.

JOE MAGARAC
and his
U·S·A CITIZEN PAPERS

by IRWIN SHAPIRO
PICTURES by James Daugherty

IF ANYBODY asks, "Who was the greatest steelman
that ever was?" you say, "Joe Magarac." And you'll be
right, by golly! Because he was the best feller for
making steel in the whole world.

Yoh! That Joe Margarac, he was a real steel man. He
was born on an ore mountain in the Old Country. He was
even made of steel himself. Sure Mike—he was solid steel
all over.

He was a big feller, too. Not so big high, maybe. Only seven or eight feet tall, about. But he was as big around as the smokestack on the steel mill. His arms were as strong as steel rails. His fingers were stronger than any other man's arms. He could never get a hat big enough, and he wore Size 18 extra-special wide-last triple-soled safety-toe shoes. Oh, he was one fine, big, strong feller.

Now some people will tell you that Joe Magarac was melted down into steel again. That was the end of Joe Magarac, they say. And he never did get his U.S.A. citizen papers.

Ho! They mean Joe Somebody-else, maybe. They don't mean Joe Magarac. They couldn't. Because Joe Magarac did get his U.S.A. citizen papers. After that, he made plenty steel for the U.S.A. You betcha your life!

Sure, he got a little bit rusty and had an accident. Sure, he fell into the ladle and was melted down. But before you hear how that happened, you have to hear about Steve Mestrovich. You see, nobody ever knew about Joe Magarac until Steve Mestrovich's party at Plotsky's farm.

So we'll start with Steve Mestrovich.

O.K. Maybe fifty, sixty, hundred years ago, Steve Mestrovich was living in the town of Braddock, Pennsylvania, U.S.A. Steve was only a little feller, but he was as proud as anything. He was proud of his bushy mustache. He was proud of being a U.S.A. citizen. He was proud of being the best cinderman in the steel mill. He was proud of the way his missus cooked. He was proud of his little house on a hill, where he could look down and see the steel mill in the valley. Most of all, he was proud of his daughter Mary.

This Mary, she was the prettiest girl in the Monongahela Valley. She had big blue eyes and goldy hair, and she could dance the polka better than anybody. All the young fellers wanted to marry her. Mary liked Pete Pussick best of all. But whenever she talked of marrying him, Steve shook his head.

"Mary," he said, "you are prettiest girl anywhere. You are daughter of me, Steve Mestrovich, best cinderman in steel mill. When you get married, you gone catch best and strongest man for hoosband."

Mary always answered, "Pete Pussick is plenty strong feller."

"I don't know about that," said Steve. "Maybe pretty soon a feller comes along who is stronger as Pete Pussick. You wait awhile, Mary. I gone have strongest man in world in my fambily."

Steve's missus folded her arms and gave Steve a look.

"Better you not be such a Smarty Aleck, Mr. Steve Mestrovich," she said.

Steve winked one eye, pulled his mustache, and snapped his red suspenders.

"Ho!" he said. "You do like I tell you. Everything gone be O.K."

So Mary waited and waited. The trouble was, no other feller came along. Everybody was getting tired of it—even Steve. But he was too proud to change his mind.

One night, though, Steve was sitting in the kitchen of his house. He was smoking a pipe, while Mary and his missus put away the supper dishes. All of a sudden there was a knock at the door—bang! bang!

202

Steve opened the door, and there stood a whole crowd
of young fellers. Pete Pussick from Braddock, Eli Stanoski
from Homestead, Andy Dembroski from Johnstown—and
a lot more. They all had fresh shaves and haircuts, and
smelled pretty like a barbershop. Some of them carried big
boxes of candy and some carried bunches of flowers. Pete
Pussick carried a box of candy *and* a bunch of flowers.

"By golly, what is this?" asked Steve. "You all come to
see Mary at one time?"

Pete Pussick took off his hat, very polite.

He said, "Mr. Mestrovich, we all bring present for Mary.
But we come to see you."

"Well," said Steve, "I am standing right here. If you
look, you see me."

All the young fellers gave Mary the candy and the flowers. Then Pete Pussick cleared his throat—ahum!—and said, "Mr. Mestrovich, for two years I come to see Mary. Eli Stanoski, same thing. Andy Dembroski, same thing. Other fellers, same thing. When we talk to you about wedding, you always say Mary gone wait to catch hoosband who is the strongest man anywhere. Now it is time for her to make up her mind."

"That is right," said Eli Stanoski. "And if you want strongest man for Mary's hoosband, don't you worry any more. Because that man is me."

"Ha!" laughed Andy Dembroski. "Eli Stanoski is good man to make talk with the mouth. But when it comes to work, that is another thing. Everybody knows I am strongest man in Johnstown mill."

"Ho!" said Pete Pussick. "Best man in Johnstown is worst man in Braddock. You want to see really strong man? Looky!"

And he picked up the icebox to show how strong he was.

"That is nothing!" yelled Eli Stanoski, picking up the stove.

"I'll show you some real muscle!" shouted Andy Dembroski. With one hand he picked up a chair with Steve's missus sitting on it.

"I'll show you both!" said Pete Pussick.

"Is that so?" said Eli Stanoski.

"You will, will you?" said Andy Dembroski.

"You betcha my life!" said Pete Pussick.

Now all the young fellers were hollering and picking up furniture. Mary giggled.

Steve's missus screamed, "Put me down!"

Steve yelled, "Don't broke up my house!"

The neighbors heard the noise and came running over.

"What is going on here?" they asked.

Pete Pussick and Eli Stanoski and Andy Dembroski all tried to answer at once. So did Steve and his missus and Mary. Everybody was making so much noise nobody could hear anybody.

At last Steve jumped up and down and gave a big holler.

"Hey!" he said. "Checkai! Stop! Shut up, everybody! And put down that furniture or I gone throw you out!"

When it was quiet again, he said, "By golly, I am tired
hearing every feller say he is right man for Mary's hoosband. I gone have strongest man anywhere in my fambily,
you betcha."

"That is what you always say," said Pete Pussick.

"Sure Mike," answered Steve. "But I joost have good idea. This Sunday I will give party at Plotsky's farm in country. Everybody come. We will have contest to find out who is really strongest man. And that feller will be hoosband for Mary."

Steve's missus folded her arms and gave him a look.

"Better you not be such a Smarty Aleck, Mr. Steve Mestrovich," she said. "What kind contest you gone have?"

Steve winked one eye, pulled his mustache, and snapped his red suspenders.

"You will see," he said. "Everything gone be O.K."

As soon as the fellers left, Steve began to get things ready for the party. He went to Pittsburgh, where he ordered two barrels of beer from the brewery. Mary helped his missus make prune jack to drink and cakes to eat. They made big pots of polnena kapusta—meat and rice wrapped in cabbage leaves.

All week everybody talked about who was going to be the strongest man. Braddock people said Pete Pussick. Homestead people said Eli Stanoski. Johnstown people said Andy Dembroski. They all wondered who would be Mary's husband.

Come Sunday, Steve and his missus and Mary went out to Plotsky's farm in the country. In a field by the river a little platform had been built. It was fixed up pretty like the Fourth of July, with flags and red, white and blue paper. Next to it stood a long table with prune-jack, the two barrels of beer, cakes, and pots of polnena kapusta. On the other side of the platform was the gypsy band from Braddock, playing fiddles. Nice sun was shining, and the people were walking around feeling good.

Steve said hello to everybody. He was all dressed up—Sunday suit, hat, necktie, everything. He kept looking at Mary, sitting next to Steve's missus. She was wearing a green and red silk dress, and she was pretty as anything.

Steve was one mighty proud feller. He winked one eye, pulled his mustache, and snapped his red suspenders.

"Hey, Eli," he said, "you feel strong today? Ho, Pete, better you have plenty steam for that contest! Say, Andy, how is your muscle?"

Along about the middle of the afternoon, Steve walked up on the platform. He told the gypsies to stop playing and held up his hand.

"All right," he said, "now I will make speech about the contest. For a long time all the young fellers want to marry my daughter, prettiest girl anywhere. Each feller say he is best and strongest man, make best hoosband for Mary. By golly, I get sick of all that talk. Now we gone find out who is really the strongest man."

He pointed to three long bars of steel in front of the platform.

"Everybody see those dolly bars from steel mill? First one weighs three hundred and fifty pounds. Second one, five hundred pounds. Third one is from bloomer mill and weighs as much as other two put together."

All the people looked at the dolly bars.

"O.K.," said Steve. "Now all you young fellers try to lift those dolly bars. The strongest and best man will be hoosband for Mary, daughter of me, Steve Mestrovich, best cinderman in steel mill, you betcha."

Everybody cheered while the young fellers stood up and took off their shirts. Most of them could lift up the first dolly bar. But the only ones who could lift up the second dolly bar were Pete Pussick, Eli Stanoski and Andy Dembroski.

211

"Now you try to lift that big dolly bar," said Steve. "By golly, that is some big hunk steel."

Eli Stanoski was the first to try. He smiled as he bent over and took a good grip on the dolly bar. He pulled and the smile came off his face. He pulled again, puffing just like a steam engine. He pulled and puffed, he puffed and pulled. It was no use. He couldn't move the dolly bar an inch.

Andy Dembroski was the next to try. First he went to the table and had a little drink of prune-jack. Then he bent over and pulled. The dolly bar didn't move. He went back to the table, had another drink of prune-jack, and pulled again. He grunted and groaned, he groaned and grunted. The dolly bar stayed on the ground.

"Come on, Pete," said Steve. "Your turn now."

Pete Pussick nodded his head. He walked all around the dolly bar. He walked around six times, maybe, looking it over. He rubbed a little dirt on his hands. He hitched up his pants. He braced his feet against the ground, bent down, and pulled. No good—he couldn't lift that dolly bar.

Pete Pussick wiped his face with a big handkerchief. Once more he walked around the dolly bar. Once more he braced his feet and bent over. Once more he pulled. This time he pulled so hard that his hands slipped and he fell down on the ground.

Before he could get up again, somebody in the crowd laughed: "Ho! Ho!"

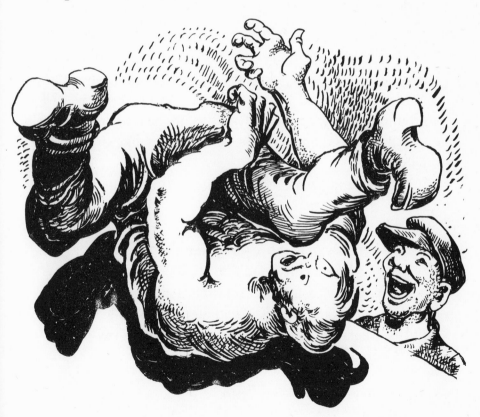

"Who is making laugh at me?" yelled Pete Pussick. "Maybe you think is easy job to lift this dolly bar. You such a strong feller, why don't you lift 'em yourself?"

"O.K.," said a voice, and a feller came walking out of the crowd.

"Looky!" said everybody. "Yoh!"

Because that feller was seven or eight feet tall, about. He was as big around as the smokestack on the steel mill. His back was almost as broad as the gate in the steel mill fence. Oh, he was some man—bigger than Pete Pussick and Eli Stanoski and Andy Dembroski or anybody. He was dressed in Old Country clothes, with a little cap on his head. His pants were too short for him, and so was his jacket.

Still laughing, he rolled up his sleeves. With one hand he took hold of the dolly bar. With the other hand he took hold of Pete Pussick. He lifted them both above his head, gave them a good shake, then put them down on the ground. Picking up the dolly bar again, he twisted it in his two big hands. Sure Mike—he twisted it like a piece of wire.

All the people watched him, their eyes and mouths wide open.

"Yoh!" they said. "Yoh!"

And they began to move away from him.

The big feller said, "Don't be afraid! I'm not hurt anybody. Joost have a little bit fun, that's all."

"Who are you, mister?" asked Steve in a small voice.

"Joe Magarac," answered the man. "That is my name—Joe Magarac."

Ho! When the people heard that, they let out one big laugh. Steve shook all over. His missus doubled up laughing. Mary giggled. Pete Pussick laughed so hard he couldn't stand up. Because in the Slovak language magarac means jackass-donkey.

"Oh, my!" said everybody. "That is some name. Joe Magarac—Joe Jackass-Donkey."

Joe Magarac smiled.

"Sure," he said. "Joe Magarac—that is me. I am big and strong and can work like magarac. I was born on ore mountain in Old Country, and I joost come to U.S.A. to work in steel mill. I am only real steel man in world. Looky, I show you."

He pulled off his shirt, and what do you think? He was made of steel all over. He thumped himself on his chest with his big fist. It made a noise like steel—bongk! bongk!

"You are joost the man I was waiting for," said Steve, taking Joe Magarac up on the platform. "You are strongest man anywhere, and you gone be hoosband for my Mary."

216

Making a little bow, Joe Magarac took off his cap to
Mary.

"By golly," he said, "you are prettiest girl I see in all my
life. But I can't be hoosband for you."

"Why not?" asked Steve.

"Joe Magarac got no time to sit around house with
missus," said Joe Magarac. "Joe Magarac work all the time,
make plenty steel. Joost work and eat, that's all. Better for
Mary to marry Pete Pussick. Next to me, he is strongest

man. And I think Mary likes him best of all."

"That is right," said Mary.

Andy Dembroski pushed his way up to the platform.

"Hey, you Steve Mestrovich!" he hollered. "If Joe Maga-rac is not hoosband for Mary, then you don't have strong-est man in world in your fambily. What do you say about that, huh?"

Steve took off his hat and scratched his head.

Then he said, "Joost a minute." Turning to Joe Magarac, he asked, "You maybe got Uncle John in Old Country?"

"No got Uncle John," answered Joe.

"You got maybe Aunt Rosie?"

"No Aunt Rosie."

"You got maybe Uncle Stanley?"

"No. No Uncle Stanley."

"You got Aunt Sophie, maybe?"

Joe Magarac nodded his head. "Aunt Sophie I got."

"Ho!" said Steve. "I got Aunt Sophie in Old Country, too. You are my cousin for sure! That's what I think all the time. So you are in my fambily, even if you don't be Mary's hoosband."

After that Steve didn't waste one little bit of time. He got a priest and an altar boy, and Mary was married to Pete Pussick. Steve gave away the bride and Joe Magarac was best man. Then the gypsies played music and everybody danced. Joe Magarac danced the polka with Mary and with Steve's missus. The people drank prune-jack and beer, and ate cakes and polnena kapusta. Everybody had a big time, you betcha. It wasn't until late at night that they started for home.

Joe Magarac asked Steve where there was a boarding-house in Braddock.

"What for you want boardinghouse?" said Steve. "You are my cousin, you come live with me. Mary will get house of her own with Pete Pussick and we will have plenty room."

"I like that fine," said Joe Magarac. "Because your missus makes the best polnena kapusta I ever taste anyplace."

Steve's missus smiled and said, "You are nice feller, Joe Magarac. I am glad you live with us."

"Sure," said Steve. "You are greenhorn joost like I was when I come from Old Country. But I will get you job in mill, U.S.A. citizen papers, everything."

So Joe Magarac went home with Steve and his missus. When they got to the house, he looked down at the steel mill in the valley. He saw the smoke pouring out of the smokestacks. He saw the red and yellow fire of the furnaces. He heard the noise of the mill and the whistle of trains.

"By golly," he said, "this is fine place! This is fine country! I gone catch U.S.A. citizen papers and be an American. Then I make best steel in world for U.S.A., you betcha your life!"

Early the next morning Steve took Joe Magarac to his foreman at the steel mill. He asked the foreman to give Joe Magarac a job.

"Well, I'll try him out," said the foreman.

Right away Joe Magarac started working on Number 7 open-hearth furnace. First he threw in ore, scrap, limestone —everything to make steel. Then he sat in the furnace door, with the fire coming up around him. As the ore melted, he stirred it with his big hands. While he worked, he sang "Columbia, the Gem of the Ocean." He didn't know all the words, so he sang it this way:

Coloombia, the Jim of the oocean!
Yoh! Hooray for the U.S.A.!

After the ore melted, he scooped up a little steel. He tasted it, blowing the steam out through his nose.

"She's cook up good," he said. "Time to tap 'em out."

Crawling into the furnace, he dumped the steel into ingot molds with his hands. He jumped out, ran to the other end of the mill, and again picked up the steel. He squeezed it through his fingers, making rails. He made eight rails at a time, four with each hand. He made rails faster and better than anybody, you betcha!

"How you like?" Joe Magarac asked the foreman.

"By golly!" said the foreman, over and over again. "By golly!"

"What I tell you?" said Steve proudly. "My cousin Joe Magarac is best steel man in world."

And the other men in the mill said, "That Joe Magarac, he is a magarac for sure."

Come payday, Joe Magarac went with Steve to a clothing store. He got him a Sunday suit, necktie, work pants, work shirts—everything. He couldn't get a hat big enough, but he bought the largest one there was. At the Star Shoe Corner he bought a pair of Size 18 extra-special wide-last triple-soled safety-toe shoes. Then he went to the store next door and bought a washtub. When he got home he fixed it up with a lid and a handle and used it for a lunch bucket. Every day Steve's missus filled it up with polnena kapusta for his lunch.

Joe Magarac had been making steel for two or three weeks, about, when one day a man came walking into the mill. He was dresed up fine, in a Prince Albert coat. He was smoking a big long cigar. Everybody worked harder than ever, because he was the superintendent of the mill. He walked along until he saw Joe Magarac making steel with his hands.

"It can't be," he said. "But it is. Isn't it?"

"Is," said Steve. "That is Joe Magarac, cousin of me, Steve Mestrovich, best cinderman in mill. He is real steel man."

"Sure, Mr. Boss Super," said Joe Magarac. And he thumped himself on the chest—bongk! bongk!

"What kind of man are you? Where are you from?" the super asked.

"Joost come from Old Country," answered Joe Magarac.

"A greenhorn, eh?"

"That is right, Mr. Boss Super. But pretty soon I gone catch U.S.A. citizen papers. Then I will be American like everybody else."

"Citizen papers, eh?" said the super. "You'll have to save up some money first. It will cost you a thousand dollars to become a citizen."

"It only cost me five dollars, Boss Super," said Steve.

The super shook his head.

"That's because you're a small man," he said. "For a big

man it costs more. Big man, big citizen—it cost more. Joe will have to pay about a thousand dollars. Turn out a lot of steel, Joe. Save your money, and by and by you'll have enough to become a citizen."

The super gave a little laugh, blew out smoke rings, and walked away.

"I think maybe Boss Super make joke," said Steve.

"Why should Boss Super make joke with greenhorn like me?" said Joe Magarac. "By golly, I got to get thousand dollars so I can catch U.S.A. citizen papers."

All day Joe Magarac worried about what to do. He worried while he ate polnena kapusta from his washtub. He worried while he cooked steel. He worried while he made rails. But when the quitting-time whistle blew, he smiled.

"Steve," he said, "I got good idea how to make plenty money for U.S.A. citizen papers. I will work day turn *and* night turn, make double money."

"When you gone sleep?" asked Steve.

"Steel man don't need sleep," laughed Joe Magarac. "Joost work and eat. Joe Magarac—that's me."

They hurried over to the foreman and asked him to give Joe Magarac an extra job. And what do you think? The foreman said no. He said he never heard of such a thing. Joe Magarac or no Joe Magarac, nobody could work day and night.

Slowly Joe Magarac and Steve left the mill. They walked up the hill to Steve's house without saying a word. They washed and sat down at the table to eat. Just as Steve's missus was bringing them a pot of polnena kapusta, Steve banged his fist on the table.

He said, "Joe Magarac, I know what you gone do. You go over to Homestead mill, catch job there, too. You don't tell them you have job in Braddock. You work day turn in one place, night turn in the other. You make double money, and you save enough for U.S.A. citizen papers."

Steve's missus folded her arms and gave Steve a look.

"Better you not be such a Smarty Aleck, Mr. Steve Mestrovich," she said. "Maybe Joe Magarac will get into trouble if he works in two mills."

"You think I will get trouble, Steve?" asked Joe Magarac.

Steve leaned back in his chair. He winked one eye, pulled his mustache, and snapped his red suspenders.

"Ho!" he said. "You do what I tell you. Everything gone be O.K."

Joe Magarac ate some polnena kapusta, then took a streetcar to Homestead. He got a job there, and after that he worked day and night. As soon as the quitting-time whistle blew in Homestead, he took a streetcar to Braddock. As soon as the quitting-time whistle blew in Braddock, he took a streetcar to Homestead. He made good steel in both places, and he saved his money to get his U.S.A. citizen papers.

Joe Magarac had been working in Homestead for two or three weeks, about, when one day the superintendent came walking through the mill. Just like the Braddock super, he was dressed up fine in a Prince Albert coat. Just like the Braddock super, he smoked a big cigar. This super didn't like to talk much. He stopped in front of Joe Magarac, looked him up and down, and said, "Hm."

The super watched Joe Magarac throw ore, scrap and

limestone into the furnace. He watched Joe Magarac cook steel, and squeeze out rails with his hands.

"Hm," he said, and walked away.

Now Joe Magarac didn't know it, but that same night the Homestead super visited the Braddock super. They sat in the parlor of the Braddock super's big house, smoking their cigars.

"I hear you're turning out a lot of steel these days," said the Braddock super.

"Hm," said the Homestead super.

"But we're turning out even more at Braddock," said the Braddock super.

"Hm?" said the Homestead super.

"That's because the Braddock steel men are the best and strongest in the world," said the Braddock super.

"Hm!" said the Homestead super.

"That's right," answered the Braddock super. "Why, I've got one man who—"

"Got a better one!" shouted the Homestead super, jumping up.

"I don't know about that."

"I do. Beat your man any day."

"And when will that be?"

"Any time you say!"

"Do you mean that?" asked the Braddock super.

"I do."

"All right," said the Braddock super. "The mills are having a picnic at Kennywood Park this Sunday. Suppose we have a little contest—your man against mine. Then we'll see which one is stronger."

"Hm," said the Homestead super, nodding his head.

The next day both the Homestead super and the Braddock super spoke to Joe Magarac. Each of them said, "Joe, how would you like to be in a little contest at the picnic? I want everybody to see how strong you are."

And Joe Magarac said to each of them, "Sure, Mr. Boss Super. I am strongest man in mill anywhere. I will win that contest for sure."

Come Sunday, Joe Magarac and Steve put on their Sunday suits. Together with Steve's missus and Mary and Pete Pussick, they started out for the picnic. Steve carried a big basket of lunch, while Joe Magarac carried his washtub of polnena kapusta.

They got on the streetcar that was crowded with people going to the picnic. The men all wore their Sunday suits. Their missuses wore white dresses. They all carried baskets of lunch, and they laughed and talked all the way.

At Kennywood Park Joe Magarac had a fine time riding on the merry-go-round and the roller coaster. After eating his polnena kapusta, he went to a big field where there was a grandstand. A band was playing, flags were flying, and the seats were filled with people.

In the front row of the grandstand sat the Braddock super and the Homestead super. Like everybody else, they were watching the men from the two mills run races. Pretty soon, though, some fellers carried in three big dolly bars. They were the same kind Joe Magarac had lifted at Steve's party. The band stopped playing and the Braddock super stood up.

"Folks," he said, "the superintendent of the Homestead mill says that Homestead men are the strongest in the world."

The Homestead people cheered, but the Braddock people went "Ho! Ho!"

The Braddock super said, "I say that the Braddock men are the strongest."

Now the Braddock people cheered, while the Homestead people went "Ho! Ho!"

"Well," said the Braddock super, "we'll see. We're going to have a little contest between the two strongest men in the mills. They'll try to lift those dolly bars, and may the best man win."

He and the Homestead super both looked at Joe Magarac.

"Ready?" they asked.

"Sure Mike," answered Joe Magarac, jumping up.

"Where's your man?" said the Braddock super to the Homestead super.

"Where's yours?" said the Homestead super.

"My man is here."

"So's mine."

"Where?"

"Right there," said the Homestead super, pointing to Joe Magarac.

"Couldn't be," said the Braddock super. "That's my man."

"He's not!" yelled the Homestead super.

"He is!" yelled the Braddock super. Then he turned to Joe Magarac. "Where do you work, Joe?" he asked. "In Braddock?"

"Sure," said Joe Magarac, "in Braddock."

The Homestead super said, "You're sure you don't work in Homestead?"

"Sure," said Joe Magarac. "Work in Homestead."

"Just where *do* you work?" asked the Braddock super. "You can't work in both places at once."

"That's what I do, Mr. Boss Super," said Joe Magarac. "Work in Braddock and Homestead. Work one place day turn, other place night turn. That way I make double money to pay for my U.S.A. citizen papers."

When the people in the grandstand heard that, they began to laugh. They pointed to the supers, laughing and slapping one another on the back. The supers' faces got red. Oh, my, they were angry as anything. They looked around at the people. They looked at each other. Then they looked at Joe Magarac.

"You're fired!" they hollered.

"Joost a minute, Boss Supers!" called Steve. "You don't want to fire Joe Magarac. He is strongest man anywhere."

"We don't, don't we?" said the supers.

"You think it over. Then maybe you won't do it."

"We won't, won't we?"

Before Steve could answer, the supers yelled, "You're fired, too!" And they left the grandstand together.

The band started playing again, but Joe Magarac didn't hear it. The sun was shining, but he didn't see it. He sat down, holding his head in his hands.

"Steve," he said, "you lose your job because of me."

"Don't you worry about that," said Steve. "But how you gone catch thousand dollars for U.S.A. citizen papers?"

People crowded around Steve and Joe Magarac. They said, "You go see Boss Super tomorrow. Maybe you get your job back again."

Steve started to walk up and down like a rooster in a barnyard.

"Why should best man in mill ask for job back?" he said. "Joe, we will go to Scranton and work in coal mine. You will be best miner in world, catch U.S.A. citizen papers, everything. Then the supers gone ask us to come back to steel mill. If we feel like, we go back. If not, not."

Oh, that Steve Mestrovich, he was some proud man!

Joe Magarac asked, "You think that will be best thing?"
Steve's missus folded her arms and gave Steve a look.

"Better you not be such a Smarty Aleck, Mr. Steve Mestrovich," she said.

Steve winked one eye, pulled his mustache, and snapped his red suspenders.

"Ho!" he said. "You do what I tell you. Everything gone be O.K."

Right away hurry-up-quick Steve and Joe Magarac got ready to leave. They said good-by to all the people. They went to Steve's house and packed their clothes. They took one look at the steel mill, then they went to the railroad station and took the train. Steve's missus went with them to make polnena kapusta.

As they rode along, Joe Magarac looked out the window. He could see the rails he had made in the mill. They were shinier than any of the other rails in the railroad track.

By and by they reached Scranton. Joe Magarac and Steve and his missus walked straight from the station to the coal mine. Miners were standing near the shaft, ready to start work. Other miners were coming out of the shaft, their faces covered with coal dust. When they saw Joe Magarac, they said, "Yoh! Looky!"

"Hello, everybody," said Steve. "This is Joe Magarac, cousin of me, Steve Mestrovich, best cinderman in steel mill. He is best man in world for making steel, and he gone be best coal miner, you betcha."

"That is right," said Joe Magarac. "I am real steel man, and I am gone dig plenty coal." And he thumped himself on the chest—bongk! bongk!

"By golly," said the miners. "Whoever heard of a steel man in a coal mine?"

"You hear about it now," said Steve. Turning to the foreman, he asked, "What you say, Boss? You got job for us?"

"Well, I'll try you out," answered the foreman.

Joe Magarac and Steve went to the company store, where they bought picks and shovels and miners' caps. Joe Magarac's cap was too small for him, but it was the biggest he could get. Picking up their picks and shovels, they went down the shaft into the mine.

It was as dark as anything in that mine. It was damp, too. Drops of water dripped down from the roof of the mine, falling on Joe Magarac. But he hardly noticed it. He was too busy mining coal. He kept digging up coal and shoveling it into carts pulled by mules. As he worked, he sang:

> *Coloombia, the Jim of the oocean!*
> *Yoh! Hooray for the U.S.A.!*

The boys driving the donkey cart sang back:

> *My sweetheart's the mule in the mines,*
> *I drive her without any lines,*
> *On the bumper I stand, with my whip in my hand,*
> *My sweetheart's the mule in the mines.*

The first day Joe Magarac worked in the mine, he dug up more coal than all the other miners. The second day he dug up as much as all the other miners. The third day he dug half as much as the other miners. The fourth day he dug as much as one of the other miners. And on the fifth day he dug half as much as any of the other miners.

When he and Steve came out of the mine, the other miners and Steve's missus was waiting for them.

"What's the matter, Joe Magarac?" asked the miners. "How come you mine such a little bit coal?"

"I am steel man," answered Joe Magarac. "Water drops down on me in mine, and it makes me rusty. I get rusty, I can't move my arms so good. That is why I dig only a little bit coal."

"Well," said the foreman, "if you can't mine coal, I'll give you a job driving one of the donkey carts."

The miners began to laugh like anything.

"Joe Magarac gone drive donkey cart like little boy!" they said. "That is good pair—mule and magarac!"

Joe Magarac hung his head.

He said, "That is all I am good for now—to work with mule. And how am I gone catch one thousand dollars for U.S.A. citizen papers?"

"Coal mine is no place for steel man," laughed the miners. "If you want to be miner, maybe you go someplace and mine steel."

"Joost a minute, joost a minute," said Steve. "That is fine idea. Joe, we will go to Minnesoota, work on Mesabi Range and mine iron ore. Then you show these fellers you are best miner anywhere."

"That sound pretty good," said Joe Magarac.

Steve's missus folded her arms and gave Steve a look.

"Better you not be such a Smarty Aleck, Mr. Steve Mestrovich," she said.

Steve winked one eye, pulled his mustache, and snapped his red suspenders.

"Ho!" he said. "You do what I tell you. Everything gone be O.K."

And right away hurry-up-quick Joe Magarac and Steve and his missus started for Minnesota. For a long time they rode on the train, but at last they got there. They went straight from the station to the open-pit mine.

Standing on a little hill, they looked down. In the ground was a big pit of red iron ore. Hundreds of men were in the pit—Finnish fellers, Slovak fellers, all kinds of fellers. Some of them dug up the ore with shovels. Others loaded it into cars that stood on tracks. Engines chugged along the tracks, pulling away the cars full of ore.

"By golly," said Joe Magarac, "that is one big hole for sure."

The miners saw Joe Magarac and ran over to have a good look at him.

"Yoh!" they said.

"He's sizable, all right," said the foreman.

"Sure, Boss," said Joe Magarac.

Steve said, "That is Joe Magarac, cousin of me, Steve Mestrovich, best cinderman in steel mill. He is most sizable man in country. He is real steel man and he is gone show you how to dig that ore."

"We'll soon see about that," said the foreman, handing Joe Magarac a shovel.

Joe Magarac shook his head.

"I don't need any shovel, Boss," he said. "I got better way."

Joe Magarac tossed away the shovel. He rolled up his sleeves and began digging ore with his hands. He dug up the ore and dumped it right into a car standing on the tracks. He was still a little bit rusty, but before long the car was loaded to the top.

All the ore miners let out a cheer.

"That is a magarac for sure," they said.

After that Joe Magarac and Steve mined ore every day. Steve's missus made them plenty of polnena kapusta, which Joe Magarac carried in his washtub.

As Joe Magarac dug up the ore, he sang:

> *Coloombia, the Jim of the oocean!*
> *Yoh! Hooray for the U.S.A.!*

The ore miners sang right back:

> *Perk your ears up, pardner mine,*
> *Cap'n coming down the line,*
> *Scratch the dirt a little more,*
> *Cover up the low-grade ore.*

Joe Magarac had been working in the open-pit mine for two or three weeks, about, when one day the foreman came over to him.

"Joe Magarac," said the foreman, "you dig up a lot of that ore. We're going to send the finest ore in the world to the steel mill in Braddock. They're going to make the finest steel in the world, for a new building for Congressmen in Washington, D.C."

"Don't you worry about that, Boss," said Joe Magarac. "I gone dig up plenty fine ore."

And he did just as he said, working faster than ever. Pretty soon, though, the sky became dark. Big, black clouds rolled up, and thunder made a noise—boom! boom! Lightning flashed, and the rain poured down. Oh, my, it rained like anything. All the ore miners put on boots and raincoats and kept on digging. But Joe Magarac just stood there, not doing a thing.

"What's the trouble?" asked the foreman.

"I think I go home, Boss," answered Joe Magarac. "If I stay out in the rain, I will get rusty."

"What!" said the foreman. "You going to let a little rain stop you? What kind of ore miner are you, anyway?"

"Joe Magarac is steel man, Boss," said Steve.

"Then let him go back to the steel mill!" yelled the foreman. "Because we've got to get that ore out, no matter how hard it rains!"

"Joe Magarac is like little baby," laughed the other miners. "When rain comes, he has to go home."

Joe Magarac nodded his head sadly and began to run. Steve ran along with him. They reached their house, went in, and sat down at the table. Steve's missus brought them some polnena kapusta, but they couldn't eat.

"What I gone do now?" said Joe Magarac. "If I mine ore in the rain, I will only be good for scrap pile. And if I can't mine ore, how will I get thousand dollars for my U.S.A. citizen papers?"

"By golly," Steve shouted, "I joost get good idea. U.S.A. government needs best steel for that Congressman building. You are best man for making steel anywhere."

"That is right," said Joe Magarac. "But how can I make steel if I am not in steel mill?"

"You listen to me," said Steve. "We will go back to Braddock. At night we will climb the fence, go into the mill, and make that steel. When Boss Super sees that good steel you make, he gone give you back your job, you betcha."

Steve's missus folded her arms and gave Steve a look.

"Better you not be such a Smarty Aleck, Mr. Steve Mestrovich," she said.

Steve winked one eye, pulled his mustache, and snapped his red suspenders.

"Ho!" he said. "You do what I tell you. Everything gone be O.K."

And right away hurry-up-quick Joe Magarac and Steve and his missus packed up their clothes. Joe Magarac picked up his washtub, and they set out for Braddock. For a long time they rode on the train, but at last they got there. It was late at night, and Joe Magarac and Steve went straight to the steel mill.

For a while they looked up at the furnaces and the smokestacks. They watched the smoke pouring out, and the red and yellow fires.

"By golly!" said Joe Magarac. "This is only place for me. Coal mine is all right for coal miner feller. Ore mine is all right for ore miner feller. But I am steel man, and steel mill is the place for me."

He leaned over, picked up Steve, and lifted him to the top of the fence around the mill. He climbed up himself, jumped down, and helped Steve to get down, too. Together they walked over to Number 7 blast furnace.

"Joe Magarac!" said the men in the mill.

"Hey! What are you doing here?" said the foreman. "You don't have a job in the mill any more!"

"Maybe I don't have job," answered Joe Magarac. "But tonight I'm gone work. I cook you up best steel in world for Congressman building."

Before the foreman could stop him, Joe Magarac began to make steel. First he threw ore, scrap and limestone into the furnace. Then he sat in the furnace door, with the fire coming up around him. As the ore melted, he stirred it with his big hands.

The foreman ran to get the super, but Joe Magarac went on making steel. He tasted a little of it, blowing the steam out through his nose.

"She's cook up good," he said. "Time to tap 'em out."

Just then the super came rushing in, yelling and hollering.

"What's going on here?" he shouted.

"Joost a minute, Boss Super," said Steve. "Everything gone be O.K. Joe Magarac, cousin of me, Steve Mestrovich, is making you best steel in world for Congressman building."

All of a sudden they heard a big splash behind them.

"Help!" hollered the men in the mill. "Get the amboolance! Get the doctor! Help!"

"What happened?" asked the super.

"Joe Magarac fall in ladle!" the men answered.

The super looked at the ladle, and what do you think? There was Joe Magarac, with the hot steel boiling up around him.

"Hello, Boss Super," said Joe Magarac. "I am still little bit rusty. I have accident and fall in."

"By golly," said Steve, "you get out or you gone be melted down yourself."

"Too late for me to get out, Steve," said Joe Magarac. "I start to melt already. But that is all right. You roll out this steel with me inside. You make girder with that steel to hold up Congressman building in Washington, D.C. It will be best girder in world, you betcha."

And Joe Magarac just sat back in the hot steel and melted a little more.

"Joe Magarac, you get out of that ladle!" yelled the super.

"Joe!" called Steve. "Hey! Checkai! Stop!"

Joe Magarac smiled and winked one eye. Then the steam hissed, the steel bubbled and boiled, and he was all melted away.

The men stood there, looking at the ladle. Slowly they took off their hats, and Steve wiped a tear from his eye. After a while the super told the men to do as Joe Magarac asked. They poured out the hot steel into ingot molds and rolled it into a girder. It was the best steel ever made, with no seam or pipe or anything. Near one end of the girder two little eyes peeped out. They were so small nobody noticed them.

The girder with Joe Magarac inside was loaded on a flatcar. All the men in the mill watched as the train started for Washington, D.C.

Steve waved his hand and said, "Goom-by, Joe Magarac. You were best steel man anywhere, cousin of me, Steve Mestrovich, best cinderman in mill. And now you are best steel girder in world."

After that the train rolled on to Washington, D.C. The girder was set up near the Capitol. Other girders were attached to it, and brick and marble were piled on. Joe Magarac held it all up. Through a chink in the marble he looked out. He could see the Capitol dome and the tall Washington Monument.

240

"By golly," he thought, "this is fine place. This is fine country. I am glad I hold up this building for Congressmen."

All through the hot summer and the cold winter Joe Magarac held up the building. He watched Congressmen and Senators coming and going. He saw the President and all kinds of people. When the cold winter was over, Joe Magarac saw the cherry trees bloom. He looked down into the street, and what do you think? There was Steve and his missus.

"Here is Congressman building," Steve was saying. "This is where Joe Magarac is in girder. He was best steel man anywhere, cousin of me, Steve Mestrovich, best cinderman in mill. How you doing, Joe? We make little trip to see Washington, D.C."

Steve winked one eye, pulled his mustache, and snapped his red suspenders. As he and his missus walked away, a Congressman and a Senator came along. They were wearing big hats and shoestring ties.

The Congressman looked at Steve and his missus.

"Foreigners," said the Congressman.

"Too many of them in this country," said the Senator.

"Just what I was thinking, Senator," said the Congressman. "We've got too many foreigners in the U.S.A.—and everybody knows they're no good."

"That's right, Congressman. These Hunkies and Bohunks—they're no good at all."

"I agree, Senator. Slovak fellers, Hungarian fellers, Russian fellers, Irish fellers, Greek fellers, Mexican fellers, Italian fellers—they're just no good."

"And Jewish fellers and colored fellers are the same."
"That's right."
"They're lazy."
"They're dirty."
"They don't talk right."
"They don't look right."
"They've got funny names."
"They've got funny ways."

"They ought to go back where they came from, Congressman."

"That's right, Senator. They're not Americans and never will be. They're not like you."

"Nor like you, Congressman."

"No, I guess we're two of the best Americans that anybody could find. And we'll have to get the foreigners out of the country."

"That's true, Congressman. There ought to be a law against 'em. What do you say we think one up?"

"Just what I had in mind, Senator. Then this country will be fit to live in."

When Joe Magarac heard that, he grew red hot with anger. He was so hot that he began to boil. As he boiled, he melted into hot steel. He melted all the way down to the ground, and the wall of the building crashed. Then he began to cool off. But he didn't turn back into a girder. He was Joe Magarac again, standing there in the middle of the bricks and marble, with a cloud of dust around him.

"Look out!" hollered the Congressman.

"Help!" yelled the Senator.

Steve and his missus heard the noise and turned around. "By golly," said Steve, "that is Joe Magarac for sure!"

Joe Magarac roared at the Congressman and the Senator: "That is right! I am Joe Magarac, that is who I am! I was born on ore mountain in Old Country, and I come to America to catch citizen papers and make best steel in U.S.A. I make plenty steel for railroads and I cook myself into girder for Congressman building. Now you say I am Hunky foreigner. You say I am no good and should go back where I came from. O.K. I go back. But if I am not good enough for you, my steel is not good enough either. So I will rip out all the steel rails I ever make. Then I go back to Old Country." And he gave himself a big, big thump on the chest—BONGK! BONGK!

"Joost a minute, Joe," said Steve. "You don't want to leave U.S.A."

"I don't stay in country where they call me names," said Joe Magarac.

With Steve and his missus running after him, Joe Magarac walked down Pennsylvania Avenue. He walked to the railroad station, then out to the railroad tracks. He looked for the rails he had made and ripped them out. He twisted them into knots and tossed them aside.

Trains stopped. Railroad fellers hollered. Steve yelled. Policemen came running up.

"Put down those rails," they said.

Joe Magarac just laughed a big laugh.

"Ho!" he said. "Who gone arrest steel man like me?"

And the policemen all backed away from him.

"By golly," said Steve. "I better do something to stop Joe. He gone broke up the whole country. I think I have good idea."

246

Steve's missus folded her arms and gave him a look.

"Better you not be such a Smarty Aleck, Mr. Steve Mestrovich," she said. "What you gone do?"

Steve winked one eye, pulled his mustache, and snapped his red suspenders.

"You come along with me," he said. "Everything gone be O.K."

Steve started back toward the Congressmen building. Joe Magarac let him go. He kept ripping up the rails and twisting them into knots. Crowds of people watched him, asking him to stop. Joe Magarac just laughed and said, "I don't stay in country like this! I don't want U.S.A. citizen papers any more! I go back to Old Country and make steel!"

Along about evening, though, soldiers came marching up—tramp! tramp! There were infantry fellers with rifles, artillery fellers with cannons, cavalry fellers on horseback. They spread across the tracks and all around Joe Magarac, surrounding him.

A general on a white horse took out his sword and said, "Joe Magarac, I order you to stop ripping up those rails."

Joe bent down and looked the general in the eye.

"Ho!" he said. "You bring whole U.S.A. Army to stop Joe Magarac. But you can't do that. How you gone shoot steel man? It not hurt me one bit."

Just then he heard Steve's voice.

"Hey! Checkai! Stop!" said Steve.

The soldiers stepped aside, making way for a carriage. In the carriage was Steve and a Congressman.

"This is Boss Congressman," said Steve. "He want talk to you."

Joe Magarac said he didn't want to listen to any more Congressmen. All the same, he did listen.

"Joe Magarac," said the Boss Congressman, "if you want

to rip up rails, I can't stop you. If you want to go back to the Old Country, I can't stop you. But before you do anything, I wish you would come with me."

"Where you gone take me?" asked Joe Magarac.

"You'll see," said Steve. "You come along, Joe. You will find out something."

"Well, all right," said Joe Magarac, getting into the carriage. They drove to the Capitol Building, went inside—and what do you think? All the Congressmen and Senators were there.

The Boss Congressman stood up before them and made a speech. He said that anybody who didn't want Joe Magarac to stay in the U.S.A. didn't know anything. He said that the Indians were the only people in the U.S.A. who didn't come from someplace else. He said that the whole U.S.A. was built up by people from the Old Country, and that the U.S.A. needed Joe Magarac to make steel. He said that anybody who helped build up the U.S.A. wasn't a foreigner any more. And he said that nobody was better than anybody else, no matter where he came from.

By golly, when he finished his speech some of those Congressmen and Senators looked mighty ashamed. Two or three of them even sneaked out of the room. Then the Boss Congressman asked everybody to vote on whether Joe Magarac should stay in the U.S.A.

"Aye!" voted the Congressmen and the Senators.

"I move we make Joe Magarac a citizen," said the Boss Congressman.

"Second the motion! Aye!" said the Congressmen and Senators.

The Boss Congressman turned to Joe Magarac and said, "Well, Joe Magarac, you can leave if you want to. If you want to go back to the Old Country we can't stop you. But the U.S.A. Congress asks you to stay and be an American."

"I don't know," answered Joe Magarac, scratching his head. "Where am I gone catch thousand dollars for citizen papers?"

"Ho!" laughed Steve. "You don't need thousand dollars, Joe. Boss Super in mill only make joke because you are greenhorn."

"That's right," said the Boss Congressman. "It wasn't a very nice joke—but that's all it was."

Joe Magarac looked at Steve. He looked at the Boss Congressman. He looked around at all the Congressmen and Senators, and then he smiled.

"O.K.," he said. "I stay."

"Hooray!" yelled the Congressmen and the Senators. They crowded around him and took him to the White House, where the President of the U.S.A. was waiting.

"Come in, Joe Magarac," the President said.

He shook hands with Joe Magarac and gave him his
U.S.A. citizen papers. Then they sat back and ate polnena
kapusta that Steve's missus had made in the White House
kitchen. A band played, and Joe Magarac danced the polka

with the President's missus. When the party was over, he
went back to Braddock.

The super of the mill said he was sorry he had played a joke on Joe Magarac. He opened the gates of the mill and people from everywhere came in to watch Joe Magarac work on Number 7 open-hearth furnace. They watched as he put in ore, scrap, limestone—everything to make steel. They watched as he stirred the steel with his hands and tasted it.

"She's cook up fine," said Joe Magarac. "Time to tap 'em out."

He poured the steel into ingot molds and squeezed out rails with his hands. Everybody cheered, and Steve was as proud as anything.

"Yoh!" he said. "That is Joe Magarac, U.S.A. citizen, best man for to make steel in world, cousin of me, Steve Mestrovich, best cinderman in mill, by golly!"

Steve's missus folded her arms and gave him a look.

"Better you not be such a Smarty Aleck, Mr. Steve Mestrovich," she said.

Steve winked one eye, pulled his mustache, and snapped his red suspenders. Joe Magarac thumped himself on the chest—bongk! bongk!

"Ho!" they said together. "You do what I tell you. Everything gone be O.K."

And that is how Joe Magarac got his U.S.A. citizen papers. And after that, he **made plenty** steel for the U.S.A. You betcha your life!